Sometime Tomorrow

D. D. Riessen

Sometime Tomorrow - Science fiction

Library of Congress Control Number: 2014935346

ISBN 10 - 0-9916630-1-2
ISBN:13- 978-0-9916630-1-9

ddr
books

San Diego, CA 92119

The professor stood at the podium, reading glasses almost falling off of the tip of his nose as he studied his notes.

After a long pause, about when the audience was beginning to fidget, he removed his glasses and leaned a bit closer to the microphone.

"If I am made up of molecules, and if those are made up of protons, electrons and neutrons, and those made up of ever smaller things, at what point do I stop being..., me?

Everything is made up of energy. Everything that we can see, measure, detect, even those things that we cannot detect but suspect that they exist, all of it is energy. It is this collection of things that we call our reality.

Gone somewhere you've never been before and recognized the place? Been introduced to somebody you've never met but already know? Know that something is going to happen before it occurs? You are not alone.

Let's talk about parallel realities...,"

To Danny

Error Code 317

East of L. A. – 2132

Anthony hardly noticed the alert when it flashed up onto the screen. Alerts come and go all the time while powering up. He pushed the Clear Alarm button thinking, "If it's bad, it'll be back."

Besides, there was something different about this run and Anthony was trying to figure out what it was. All views of the probe appeared normal, all power readings were normal. Normal, normal, normal, yet..., "What do you think, Malcolm? Sound different?"

Malcolm turned up the volume and leaned toward the speaker, as if another six inches was going to make a difference. "Smoother. It sounds smoother. That's the word that comes to mind."

"Agreed. But..., why? What's changed since our last run? All we did was replace two defective power packs. That shouldn't make any difference."

As was his habit when events were going differently than expected, Malcolm leaned back in his chair and buried his hands into the waterfall of thick red hair that covered all but the top of his head. "What's that alert on your screen?"

Anthony cleared alarms a second time. The screen momentarily went blank and then the alert reappeared. "We've got an error code 317. What is that?"

Malcolm queried his screen. "Let's see, error code 317. Says it's an error in thruster four, composite frequency invalid."

This time it was Anthony that upped the volume. Low frequency rumbling from the probe's thrusters vibrated through the room as the sounds slowly

1

built into a roar. "Error code's not clearing, Malcolm. Let's shut it down and check it out."

"What are we at? Fifty percent power?"

"Fifty-three and climbing. Jordan should see this on his screen. Why isn't he initiating an abort?"

"Sounds better," said Malcolm, wanting to let it go a little longer. "Like it's finally doing what it's supposed to do."

"You've got an alarm that doesn't clear. I suggest we abort until we know why."

The door opened and Lindy stuck her head inside. "Sorry I'm late. Everything going OK?"

Anthony glanced over at Malcolm. "No. We have an abnormality. We need to shut it down."

"Lindy," said Malcolm, turning in his chair. "Does the probe sound different to you?"

She stepped into the room and closed the door behind her. "Sounds better, smoother. What did you do?"

"Smoother or not," Anthony replied, his face reddening. "Until we know what's causing the error code, we need to stop."

Malcolm leaned over to check Anthony's monitor. "What's his power now?"

"Seventy and climbing."

Malcolm found his cup, swirled the remaining coffee around, hoping to get the last of the sugar at the bottom. "He'll stop at eighty. It's in the program."

"That's what it's supposed to do," said Anthony. "But that alarm might change everything. Jesus, Malcolm. Abort the test!"

Lindy leaned down over Anthony's shoulder, studying the monitor. "Seventy-eight percent now."

Another warning flashed up onto the screen advising that the probe was now under manual control. The roaring sound screamed up into a high whining whistle and then blasted into something far beyond human hearing. A blinding flash of white light filled the room, and then the entire testing area went black.

Bells, ringing into the darkness, one steady unrelenting ring, accompanied by a highly irritating buzzer, two short blasts on, one off, echoing throughout the concrete bunker, two stories down, letting everyone know that something was wrong.

Anthony rubbed his eyes, hoping to see something other than the bright blue after-flash. "Damn it! Sucked the juice right out of us." Attempting to find the handle of the drawer where he kept a flashlight, he knocked over his coffee.

"Ventilation's down," said Malcolm, feeling the sudden loss of cool air coming in from the ceiling. "Where's back-up?"

"It has a time delay," said Lindy, standing between Malcolm's and Anthony's chairs, holding onto the backs of them until some kind of light came on. "The program has to ensure it's safe before it turns on the power."

Anthony opened the drawer and fumbled around with the contents inside. "At least they could turn off the fricking bells! We know there's a problem."

As the lights slowly flickered on, cool air flowed back into the tiny room, the computers came back to life and the bells fell silent.

"Got a shit load of alarms," said Anthony as he watched them scroll down his screen.

Malcolm flipped through all of the different perspectives of Eclipse on his monitor, each view accompanied by a short inhalation of disbelief until he was on his feet, looking out through the tinted glass hoping the cameras were wrong, malfunctioning, taken out by the blast. And then he fell back into his

3

chair. "Probe's gone. Jesus."

Lindy put her hand on Anthony's shoulder, leaned forward and gazed out the window, staring quietly at the empty space.

How odd? Something so sleek and beautiful can be there one second and gone the next.

No smoke. No steam. Just..., gone.

"Where's Jordan? Do we have communications?"

Anthony paused the listing of alarms and read one in particular. "Security alert. We got ourselves a rat. I think we'd better go into lock down."

Lindy pulled the strap back up over her shoulder and stepped through the doorway onto the SwiftLine. She seated herself mid-car, secured her belongings, did a quick take of everybody else inside and, feeling pretty sure that she hadn't been followed, pulled out her LifeLink and called Adelle, back at the condo.

"Yes, Miss Lindy?"

"Adelle. I am instructing you to go to Level Four."

"Please enter password."

Lindy held the LifeLink in front of her face and thought out the password. A blinking green dot appeared down in the right hand corner, accepting the code.

"I am now operating under the programming of Level Four, Miss Lindy. I am accessing your Cond-Orbit account and preparing to transfer all assets to the pre-programmed destination. Should I continue?"

"Yes."

"Miss Lindy, that set of instructions is now being implemented. I am now accessing your computer to complete the pre-programmed set of instructions. Should I continue?"

"Yes."

"Computer accessed. Delete all files, Miss Lindy?"

"Yes."

"Delete all passwords, and codes used to access secure links, Miss Lindy?"

"Yes. Delete everything. Take the computer down to basic so that there is no memory of me."

"Miss Lindy, your assets are being transferred and I am now de programming the computer."

"Adelle, when that task is complete, you will revert

back to your basic model. You will allow yourself to be programmed up to Head of Household, but you will not allow yourself to be programmed beyond that, except for me."

"Yes, Miss Lindy."

"And you will go into hibernate until someone inputs your life code."

"Yes, Miss Lindy."

"I will be calling in from time to time. Answer those calls and await my instructions."

"Yes, Miss Lindy. The computer task will be completed within five minutes. Anything else, Miss Lindy?"

"That is it. Goodbye, Adelle."

"Goodbye, Miss Lindy. It has been a pleasure serving you."

Lindy cleared the call and attempted to gain access into Project Eclipse. Denied.

Of course it's denied. Something happened. Something big. Did it work? Is Jordan alive? Did he make it back? Or, did the whole thing just blow up and disintegrate?

Got our selves a rat. That's what Anthony said. How did he know? What kind of security alert? Thought I'd at least be able to stick around and see what happened.

Damn you, Jordan! Why didn't you let me know?

Using a mirror and pretending to apply lipstick, Lindy studied the other passengers in the car, the woman in a business suit that looked like she drank too much and led an unhappy life, a man sitting across the aisle from her, checking out the woman's legs, wondering if he should give it a shot, the two young executives in cheap suits talking excitedly about some deal they'd just made, the creep looking up over his papers checking her out.

Lindy abruptly turned and glared at the man with a look that said, "Try anything, jerk-off and you'll be minus a pair." He looked away.

Lindy knew she was beautiful. She had naturally blonde hair, which she kept short and styled, dark eyes that men thought they could read, the fools, high Aryan cheekbones, sensual lips and a body that burned sex. Yes. Men always looked. She was used to that. But today she was not in the mood.

The SwiftLine pulled into the station and the doors slid open, a muffled whoosh. Lindy gathered her things and headed for the exit.

Another two minutes and I'll be out of here. I wonder if they've figured it out.

My God, Jordan! You could've told me! Thought I had your trust.., bastard.

Tess

Tess knew what she had to do. She retrieved Ellie's phasor from under the carved out tree stump that she used for a chair, tucked it into her belt and turned to follow the others.

One of them was wounded, his left arm in a sling and blood coming through the bandages around his chest. Ellie must have done a number on him.

Ellie's hands were tied behind her back and attached to the rope wrapped around her waist, the other end of which was tied to the belt of a stocky, bearded man who was wearing a worn, drooping canvas hat.

They had stopped near the edge of a bluff and were checking out the land below, two of them pointing and discussing the trail heading back down while the third was busy tending to his wounds.

With heart pounding, ears ringing, Tess took a deep breath, pulled out the phasor, released the safety and wondered which one to shoot first.

She didn't know how to use it, or if it would recoil, or how much power to set it for. Ellie had used level one to stun rabbits. Tess turned the dial to ten and aimed at the one attached to Ellie. Better to shoot him first and give her a chance to get away.

A bit of movement out of the corner of her eye. The wounded man had spotted her and was drawing his weapon. Instinctively, she aimed at him and pulled the trigger...,

Ramon appeared, coming into her bedroom from the hallway.

"Miss Tess. Jordan is calling."

"Jordan? That's odd. Haven't heard from him since forever."

Watching herself answer the call, as if looking down from some invisible perch up near the ceiling she saw herself putting him up on the monitor.

"Hey, Tess. Got a minute?"

"Jordan?"

"This is an emergency. Please listen...,"

The lights turned on. Rolling over onto her back, pulling the covers with her, Tess found herself lying in bed, wide-awake, wondering what had just happened. "A dream," she was thinking. "Just a dream."

No time to dwell on it. Off to work. Got places to go, things to do, an early meeting and reports to get out. It's always a long day and dark when she gets home...,

The light came on as Tess approached her doorstep. "Hi, Ramon."

Inside, Ramon snapped out of hibernate, opened the door and let her in. "Welcome home, Miss Tess. There are three messages needing your response. A package has arrived, unexpected. It had your code on it, so I accepted it."

"Where is it?"

"In the back room. I've scanned it for poisons, radiation and explosives. It appears harmless."

"It is. It's a lamp."

"A lamp?"

"Yes, from an antique shop. It was in the window. Bring it out here and we'll open it."

Tess sat, removed her shoes and let her hair down while Ramon retrieved the package. He set it next to her chair and handed her a knife, which she used to cut the tape. Carefully, she pulled back the packing.

"See? It's a bronze sculpture with four human faces. And they're holding a crystal ball between them."

Ramon ran his scanner over the lamp. "This is a

very old process, forging brass as they have. And those are human faces? Why do humans do that, make objects in their own image? It's irrational, and certainly not functional. The faces have no light distribution qualities at all."

"It adds to the beauty of the lamp, Ramon. I don't expect you to understand that."

"I was having trouble with it, Miss Tess."

"The back sides of the faces hold the crystal in place. See? They form a ring. So, they do have some function."

"The crystal ball makes no sense either. I see markings etched into the side, but I cannot identify the hieroglyphics."

"Hmm. Me either. I didn't see that when I bought it."

"Incoming message," said Ramon. "It's from Malcolm."

"Put him on. Deny outgoing video."

Malcolm flashed up onto the screen. "Hey, Tess. Are you terribly busy, right now?"

"Hi Malcolm. No. Just got back from a trip down south. I managed to...,"

"The reason I ask is because we have an emergency here at the lab. Can you come in right away?"

Malcolm's voice had an urgency to it that told Tess not to say no. He was worried about something and wasn't going to say what over an open line.

"I'm on my way, Malcolm. I'll be there within the hour."

Tess got up with a sigh. "Ramon. Store the lamp at the foot of my bed. Do not plug it in. But first, get me a clean set of clothes and prepare a sandwich and coffee for me to go."

"Yes, Miss Tess."

The dome itself, ten miles in diameter, was made of rigi-flex poly carbonate solar panels that were programmed to flex with the earthquakes, filter the sun's rays, collect solar energy and to keep the dome's temperature at a constant seventy-two degrees.

The heat from the enormous flow of current into the storage system was run through heat exchangers that provided all of the hot water necessary for living under the dome and steam to drive the generators that provided power for vast electrical needs of day to day operations inside the dome.

Tess let the reader scan her eyes and mentally thought out the code. When the security door clicked open, she headed down the stairs to the SwiftLine, where she programmed in Stop 4.

Normally, she preferred to travel above ground, slower, but because it was used for shipping, receiving, basic construction personnel, and the general visiting public, wealthy customers coming to purchase one of the company's orbiting modular homes, the trip was far more interesting.

Tess got off at the fourth stop, hurried down the long, main hallway, made a right at the second corner and followed that to the end, Malcolm's office. He was pacing the floor when she came through the doorway.

"Hey, Tess. Thanks for dropping everything. We've got a serious problem on our hands."

Tess smiled. Malcolm was one of those people that would always have a serious problem. Maybe it was his sharp pointed nose going one way and his thick, wavy, highly receded head of red hair always pointing backward, that made her think of a profoundly concerned wind vane.

If the shipments didn't arrive on time or if they were of low quality, or if the projects were behind schedule, or if something wasn't working right, Malcolm would point his head and go investigate. Malcolm would suffer from a heart attack or stroke sometime soon.

"Hey, Malcolm. You sounded worried. What's up?"

"Do you remember Jordan Blake? He was in your department a while back. He helped build the revised prototype for the two human orbiting condo."

"Yes. And then he transferred into Research and became a test engineer."

That was when Tess learned that there was more to Jordan than met the eye. Besides her, he was also seeing a woman in that department, Lindy Moore, one of the design engineers working on that project. Confronted with that, Jordan dumped Tess. He came home one night and out of the blue said it was over, grabbed a few things and was gone.

Malcolm poured himself another cup of coffee and held out an empty cup for Tess with a questioning look.

"No, thanks."

"He's been doing very well in that department. They are working on an orbiting community hub, a place where people can shop, dine, and get together. One of the things they've discovered is that, as wonderful as living in orbit is, people still feel a need to socialize. There are going to be whole communities up there, places where you lock in your condo, buy a parcel in space and have access to other communities. Cities are being built and there's a fortune in that. It's the new frontier."

"What's this got to do with me?"

"Jordan was also working on an experimental craft. And before I go any further, I have to remind you that what you are about to hear is for your ears only. You know the rules that apply, correct?"

"Of course."

"Jordan was involved with a craft that had no propulsion, Project Eclipse. It carried only the necessities for survival."

"No propulsion at all? How does it maneuver, once it's in orbit?"

"It never leaves the room."

"Oh. Like suspended animation?"

"Sort of. The craft is designed to probe a parallel reality."

Tess walked over to the coffee pot and poured herself a cup, grabbed a donut from what looked like snacks from a meeting earlier in the day. And then she found a comfortable chair to sit in. "*What?*"

"It's a vehicle that resonates at several different wavelengths simultaneously. The idea is to create matter that is different than what is available in this universe."

"I don't see how that can work. If it doesn't go anywhere...,"

"It doesn't have to. We're combining energy in ways that allow atoms to interact differently, a quantum approach. We won't go into the details. That's not why you're here."

"Why am I here?"

"We know you had an affair with Jordan. And that he was subsequently involved with a woman, Lindy Moore. Unfortunately, she was also working for someone else."

"Was?"

"Still is, apparently. She escaped from the dome before we could talk to her."

13

"With Jordan?

"No. We know he wasn't with her. We need your help locating him."

"We haven't been together for..., I don't know, half a year? Longer than that, I think. We haven't spoken for the last several months. I have no idea what he has been doing."

"He still loves you."

Tess laughed. "Riiight."

"He's also a special agent for the government. He was on assignment to watch Lindy. Turns out, she was also an agent, but not for us."

"OK. You're asking me to believe an awful lot of what, for the time being anyway, I'm calling hearsay. Where is Jordan?"

"We don't know."

"He must've gone with Lindy."

"No. He and the probe disappeared into thin air, right in front of the cameras."

"Wait." Tess sipped her coffee, contemplating the meaning of that last statement. "Does that mean the experiment *worked*? Is he in some sort of..., where is he?"

"We don't know. We've lost communications with the probe."

"OK. Wait. Why was Jordan *in* the probe? Don't you normally send mice for things like that? Work your way up to monkeys? And then, when you get the bugs all worked out, some foolhardy human, and yes, Jordan is one of those, heads out with a song and a prayer."

"We needed human input. What can a rat tell us about parallel realities?"

"For one, whether or not something going there from here can survive. What was the plan for his return?"

"When he's ready to return, a signal is sent and we reverse the process. That puts him back here on the stand."

"If he was going into..., what was he going into? Parallel reality? What does that actually mean?"

"A time and place that exists right here with us. The probe's still on the launch stand as far as we know. We just can't detect it."

"How were you going to communicate? Would he even have a probe over there? And I still don't know what this has to do with me. Like I said, we haven't talked for months. We've both moved on."

"He has five days left."

"Before what?"

"The probe is in a high energy state and if it doesn't touch down *on* the stand, possibly a violent reaction when he returns, depending on what he lands on."

"And Jordan dies?"

"Most likely."

"I thought you said the probe never leaves the stand."

"In theory. But without tracking, we can't be sure. It might drift off target. We don't know the relationship of parallel realities. Are they constant with respect to our time and space? Do we drift apart and realign? What kind of glue holds us together? Or, are we totally unrelated? The instruments in the probe are designed to answer some of those questions."

"Again. What's this got to do with me?"

"Jordan was very impressed with a holographic memory system that you designed. He was working on ways for the system to be interactive with humans."

"Hmm. Without my permission."

"He called your work the first true artificial intelligence, programmable behavior that develops into a personality as it gains knowledge."

"OK, Malcolm. You're getting off on a tangent. What's this got to do with me?"

"He installed a telepathy transducer into the probe and was building the other end of it, programmable intelligence, here in the lab. He claimed that it would be capable of telepathy. He wasn't done working on it."

"My God, Malcolm, get to the point. What's this got to do with me?"

"You understand the memory side of it. We don't. The communications part is relatively basic, the telepathy transducer. I'd like for you to get the holographic memory part of it working. And then we want you to call Jordan."

"And tell him what, to come home? I'm pretty sure that's already on his mind."

"Last we saw, he was in manual control. The first thing would be to help him get the probe back under computer control. Failing that, give him coordinates that he can program into the onboard database."

"Shouldn't that information already be there?"

"Yes." Malcolm shrugged. "He's supposed to be able to communicate once he lands in some other reality. That should be within a second, or two. Either...," and here he paused, working his hands as if they were going to mold a solution, "he hasn't landed or communications are out because there is no tracking."

"Or, he's already dead. What if I don't want to do this?"

"Personally, Tess, you're one of our best engineers and I don't want you leaving your current project. But this is your chance to jump into the experimental side, where engineering leaps toward the conceptual. I think you'd like that."

"How odd. I'm being asked to help save the one person I really don't want to see again."

Zodi stared at the meter in disbelief. The power reading had been three hundred and twenty. She had read it, made a mental note of it just like she'd done a thousand times before, but dropped her pen when she went to write it down.

The pen hit the floor and bounced beneath the equipment rack.

Isn't that how it always goes? Drop something and it never fails to go behind something else and find the darkest corner.

Why? The odds should be fifty-fifty that it lands out in the open.

First on her hands and knees and then flat out on her belly, Zodi finally got her fingertips on the pen, used her fingernails to spin it within reach and pulled it in.

Standing, she double-checked the meter. She expected three-twenty but it had gone up to four-eighty.

What? This stuff is steady. It never goes up or down more than fifty. Yet...,

A loud hum began to fill the tiny room as the meter indicated ever larger energy consumption, four-eighty, five-sixty..., fans, converters, multi-plexers, anything electrical, whirring itself into a gigantic mechanical roar.

The room, all four hundred square feet of it, heated up as if a warm desert wind had just blown through, even though the door to the outside was closed and the air-conditioning was on. And then, slowly, the sounds in the room drifted back down to normal.

Seconds later, Adan flung the main entrance door open and peered inside. "What *was* that? Sounded like a tornado just came through!"

Zodi was studying the power rack above her, the large one that spanned the room, looking for smoke. "No idea. Whatever it was, it's gone now."

"It's warm in here."

"Temperature's normal. I just checked it. Sixty-eight." She glanced over at the gauge on the wall. "Wait. Look at that. It's up to eighty! It was sixty-eight. I wrote it down no more than a couple of minutes ago. Strange."

"I heard a crackling sound up on the antenna tower," said Adan. "Like something shorted out. Didn't see any sparks though. You feel OK?"

"I'm fine. What was that?"

Adan started to back out of the doorway. "Don't know. Let's finish up and get out of here."

"We report it?"

"Report what? It was weird for a second or two, but now everything's OK?"

"Well, something happened. And if something with that kind of power is inside the dome with the rest of us, someone needs to know about it."

"Let's just finish up and go," said Adan, as he closed the door.

Alarmology

Pierce removed his glasses, leaned back in his chair and rubbed his eyes. "God, that screen drives me crazy! You would think, after all these years, that they could come up with something better than that." He pulled at the short hairs covering his chin, as was his habit after cutting his beard too short. He didn't like the bristle.

Standing next to him, patiently waiting, Joe glanced over at the reader on the shelf next to Pierce. "Yet, you refuse to use the scanner."

"Because I don't want that thing reading my mind. I don't know what else it's looking at."

"It only reads conversation."

"That's what they say. Who are they, anyway?"

Pierce got up, stretched backwards with a groan, and then searched the room for his coffee.

"Over there," said Joe, pointing to the cup sitting on the desk.

Pierce retrieved his coffee, maneuvered around his desk and sat down. "So, you've got random alarms. What are you going to do about them?"

"The whole system tests OK. I suggest that we install a second, more conventional system and run it parallel to this one."

Pierce opened the drawer on his left, removed a folder and centered it in front of him, smiling at the thought that he was probably the only person in the dome that still used paper.

Something tangible about paper. Nobody can make changes but me.

"Cost?"

"Unknown. I need approval to proceed. Certainly cheaper than replacing all of the existing, sophisticated hardware, just on suspicion. It's only happened twice."

"Let me ask you this. Say..., both systems show an alarm. And they go off at the same time, what would that prove?"

"That someone or something is in the room. But that would be odd. The outside wall is reinforced concrete, no windows or doors. There is a small ventilating fan to the outside but it's too small for anything to get through. Besides, there are two screens and a filter inside that air shaft and they haven't been tampered with. The rooms on either side of the Testing Center are...,"

"I know, Software and Staging. Both have access doors. Did either room sound an alarm?"

"No. The only other access into the room is from the hallway and that is secured on both ends. No alarms in the hallway either. It must be a fault in the system. Otherwise, something, whatever it was, would have to materialize *inside* the room."

"That would be odd, wouldn't it? Cameras didn't pick up anything?"

"Nothing."

"Say you put in the new system. If we get an intrusion alarm on the new system and the old one doesn't pick it up, what would that prove?"

"That the old system is defective."

Pierce sipped his coffee. "What if the alarm goes off on the old system and the new system doesn't detect anything? What does that prove?"

"Then..., the old alarm system must be defective. It will have gone off three times when there's nothing there."

"It seems like, no matter what, the existing system is defective, in your mind."

"I see your point. Thank you. So, abandon the

idea?"

"No. Put it in. I want to see what happens. Let me know when they're both up and running."

"Yes, sir."

Dorian Zimmer

Dorian Zimmer placed a call to Malcolm, the project manager for the testing of prototypes back on earth, and then settled in on his couch, faced the screen, and readjusted his fedora.

Dorian did not like that he was balding. He had tried the lotions, the massages, the hair transplants, hypnosis, gene therapy, psychic healing, most anything anybody suggested. But the fact of the matter was that his head did not want any hair, at least nothing higher than an inch above his ears all the way around.

So he wore hats, cowboy hats, baseball caps, French berets, anything to cover his head, not that he needed protection from the sun, not while living in his condo three hundred miles above Earth. All light entering his abode was filtered.

Dorian's job was to keep the expansion of Cond-Orbit's new orbiting community center on track. It was the docking centers that were causing the most problems.

The drivers of the handy little Go-pods, included with every condo, didn't know how de-accelerate properly and were damaging the landing pads. The crews were spending more time repairing the existing pads than they were installing new ones.

With business flourishing, condos selling faster then they could be integrated into the community, and the new weekly shuttle to and from Earth, always bringing more people up than taking them down, Dorian could see that something needed to be done.

Malcolm's image flashed up on the screen. Seeing the hat, Malcolm smiled. "Hey, Dorian. I like your hat."

Dorian nodded a thank you. "If I had your hair, Malcolm, I wouldn't need a hat."

"Keeps me moving," said Malcolm, running his fingers through the anxious wisps. "Like an air foil." He smiled. "So..., Dorian, what's up? I know you don't call unless you want something. What is it that I have that you want?"

"A couple of things. Corporate notified all of us this morning, said there was some kind of mishap inside the dome?"

"Is this line secure?"

"All lines on this link are secure."

"You are familiar with Project Eclipse?"

"I've been following it since its inception. Actually, it's my department that's tracking the funding. I've only seen images of the probe, though."

"Well..., it's gone."

"Gone. Gone away? Blew it self up? What?"

"The test engineer went to full power during what was supposed to be a limited power test. The craft launched..., disappeared."

"Hmm," Dorian readjusted his hat back on his head. "Is that what it's designed to do?"

"Yes. But..., we were not ready for a full power run. It looks like the engineer put the probe into manual at the last second and took it full power. Why, we don't know."

"Do you have communications with him?"

"Unfortunately, no. And that's the problem. If we can't communicate, we can't coordinate locations, power differences, homing signals, you know."

"So..., according to what I've been reading, other than loss of communications, is this what the probe was supposed to do?"

"Yes."

"And you don't know when, or if, it's coming back?"

Malcolm shrugged. "If we can't communicate, we can't coordinate. It may never come back."

Dorian laughed. "That's a tough one, Malcolm. How are you going to write that up in the accident report?"

"What accident? We can't say Jordan's dead because we don't know. And we can't say the probe is missing. We just don't know how to talk to it."

"That's why I like to keep my hands on the tangible things. I pray this never happens, but if one of my condos floats away, I'll know where it went. Good luck to you. I'm glad that's not my problem."

"And what is your problem? You called me."

"We're having trouble keeping up with production. My engineers are telling me that the inter-compartment seals are not fitting properly and that they're having to spend a lot of extra time making them work. Can I get you to run a quality check, make sure they're being made to spec?"

"I'll pull three random samples out of shipping and get back to you soon as I know something."

"Thanks, Malcolm."

"Anything else?"

"Yea. The crazy drivers from LA are now moving up here. We need to come up with a reinforced entrance to the landing pads, something that will hurt their craft more than our pads. Got any ideas?"

"That's an easy one, Dorian. I'll put a couple of engineers on it. I wish my problems were that simple. If you see a probe floating by, let me know, will you?"

Dorian laughed. "I'll keep my eyes peeled. Thanks, Malcolm."

Ramon uttered a quiet "Ahem," when he approached Tess, who was busy studying the materials that Malcolm had given her to look over.

Look over is such an inadequate phrase. What he meant was, drop everything. Study this until your head can't take in any more. Practice until you can perform the operations in your sleep. Allow the program to read your mind. He's out there somewhere. Go get him, Tess.

A second, "Ahem," from Ramon caused her to look up.

"Yes, Ramon?"

"Miss Tess. There are two agents at the door that would like to speak with you."

"Who are they?"

"The man's name is Drake Walker. The woman's name is Vivian Bustworthy."

"What do they want?"

"They say that they are from the Department of Interior. They would like to speak with you about Jordan Blake."

"Department of Interior? Put them on the screen. Deny video-out."

"Yes, Miss Tess."

Drake appeared uncomfortable in the slacks and sports jacket that he was wearing and looking like he was going to be strangled by the tie. His hair was cropped short, barely enough to part and comb to one side. He looked like an athlete, with his square jaw and big chest.

Vivian was the opposite of all of that. If her name had anything to do with her appearance, it was wrong. She had few, if any, curves. And her dress, closed at the top with a collar that hid half of her neck, fit her form perfectly all the way down to just above her knees. Looking over the top of her glasses, she spoke to the camera.

"Tess Altman?"

"Speaking. How may I help you?"

"We are with the U.S. Government." She held her badge up to the camera for Tess to see. "If you don't mind, we'd like to ask a few questions about Jordan Blake. May we come in?"

Tess didn't like the feel of it. "What department did you say you were with?"

"Department of Interior."

"FBI?"

"No. We are..., a little less known. We're with the Department of Interior, Special Operations."

"And what is it that you do?"

Vivian Bustworthy appeared put off by the questioning, a furrowed brow and pursed lips. "Miss Altman, I can assure you that we are legitimate. We would just like to ask you a few questions about Jordan Blake."

"I'm not objecting to that, yet. I'm just not used to cold calls. Both of you appear out of nowhere wanting access into my house. What is it that you want to know about Jordan Blake?"

"It's a private matter, something we should not be discussing through an unsecured comm. system."

Tess muted sound and glanced over at Ramon. "Let them in. Do not allow access to any part of the house except the front room."

"Yes, Miss Tess. Should I go to Code Two?"

"Code Two? Oh. Heightened security? Sure. Go to Code Two and stay in the room with us."

"Yes, Miss Tess."

Ramon was a comfort, just being around. He was

like a little kid, wanting to know about everything, asking questions. His duties were to answer messages, clean the house, cook and he was eager to engage Tess in conversation when she allowed it. He was also an electronic guard dog.

Craftsman style furniture had come back into vogue, only without using real wood. Tess had purchased an imitation wood love seat and chair with matching style coffee table which, after moving them around a bit to get them to fit into the eight foot by ten foot room, worked fairly well when meeting with visitors, that in itself, a rare occasion.

Ramon scanned both of them as they came through the door, circling behind them as they entered the room, and then he stopped next to the doorway leading into the hall. Tess checked their identification and motioned for them to sit. Drake declined. Vivian sat in the chair. Tess seated herself so that she faced Vivian.

"I'm sorry for the inconvenience," said Vivian, with a quick smile. "But we would like to ask a few questions about Jordan Blake."

"Such as...?"

"If you can remember the last time, the exact date if you can, that he was here."

Tess leaned back into her chair. "How do you know that he was ever here?"

"Our records show that for approximately six months Jordan lived at this address. We also know that, during that time, he was not staying at his place with Cond-Orbit."

"How do you know this?"

"Cond-Orbit likes to keep tabs on some of their very special employees."

"And yet you are from the government? I don't understand the connection."

"Cond-Orbit has several contracts with the government. There have been some problems developing over a period of time and we're attempting to determine when they began. If it was after he moved away from here, then we can eliminate you as a suspect."

"I'm a suspect?"

"We're covering all bases. That's why we would like to hear the actual date, if you can remember."

"If I give you a date, I'm admitting that he was here. And I don't know why I should give you that information."

"Miss Altman, we have the authority to arrest you and charge you with sabotage against the U.S. Government. We can also get a search warrant and tear the place apart. We especially like visiting in the wee hours of the morning. How would you like to proceed?"

"I need to make a call," said Tess, getting up and leaving the room. "I'll be right back. Would either of you like a glass of water?"

"No, thank you," Vivian smiled. Drake nodded no with a stiff smile.

Tess did not know what else, exactly, Code Two meant and made a mental note of it to find out later. But if they started to drift down the hallway, they would be surprised to find themselves dealing with a talking robot that blocked their way. She input Malcolm's number.

"Malcolm here."

"Malcolm, why is it that two agents are here in my house asking questions about Jordan?"

"What? Who are they?

"Vivian Bustworthy and Drake, I think his last name was Walker."

"Never heard of them. Whom do they work for?"

"They're claiming Department of Interior, Special

Operations."

"What do they want to know?"

"So far, all they want is the date that he moved out. They've threatened to search the place if I don't cooperate. No idea what they think they're going to find."

"Let me ask you this. When Jordan lived there, did he ever bring his work home with him?"

"He did do a lot of conceptual work here. He set up a small studio in the spare room, worked on his drawings, and he was always working on some kind of calculations. He took all of that with him when he left."

"Give them the date. If that gets them off your back, the information was worth it. If they keep pressing, well, call me back. Bye."

Tess retrieved her LifeLink from the bedroom, returned to the front room and sat down. "I believe that it was back in March. Here it is, March sixteenth. That was the last time he was in my house."

"You are sure of that?"

"Yes. That was the day that he picked up the last of his things. I had it scheduled for ten in the morning. I wrote that he was half an hour late and was gone by eleven-fifteen."

"Miss Tess, this is Ramon. I would like to warn you that the male is carrying an RX700 Phasor. I do not have a defense for that type of weapon."

Tess stared at Ramon, jaw dropping slightly. Those words had been received inside her head. The robot had not spoken. Nor had he moved.

"How long have you known Jordan?"

"Jordan? Oh..., about a year. I met him when I first came into that department. But it was three months before we started dating."

"I see. Did he have other visitors while he was stay-

30

ing here?"

"Miss Tess, the female is recording this conversation, which is illegal without your consent. I have the ability to destroy her recording without her knowing it. Shall I proceed? Please nod yes, or no. I am operating under the programming of Code Two, at your request."

Tess nodded a very slight no. "I'm sorry. What was the question?"

"Did he have other visitors while he was here?"

"No. We were very private."

"Do you know if he ever brought any classified documents here into this house?"

"He kept his work at work. And it's impossible to get classified documents through Security. What has Jordan done?"

"I'm afraid I cannot answer that question."

Tess wanted very much to ask what they knew of the program. But even hinting that she had any kind of knowledge of that would surely put her in somebody's interrogation room, at the least, stuck in another, much stiffer round of questions.

"Do you know the whereabouts of Jordan's personal computer?"

"I have no idea. The only things left in this house that came from Jordan are the wine glasses. There were four. I'm down to three. Broke one."

"Did he communicate with Cond-Orbit while staying here?"

"I suspect that you already know that. Yes. He did. I have a secure link into Cond-Orbit because of the nature of my work. Sometimes Jordan used that line, but he had his own passwords and levels of security."

Ramon whirred to life. "There is an incoming priority call." *"Miss Tess, the call is from Malcolm."*

Tess stood. "Excuse me, please. I need to get this."
She picked up the call in her bedroom. "Hello?"

"How's it going, Tess?"

"I'd like to stop giving them information."

"Right. The reason I called is that we have an emergency at work and we need for you to come in and help..., now."

Tess smiled. "I'm on my way."

Jonas Von Darr removed his sunglasses and carefully cleaned them with his handkerchief, holding one lens at a time by the sides. "Our probe doesn't work. Please help me to understand why."

"Excuse me." Lindy smiled, and then stood and moved her chair so that she could sit in the shade of a group of potted pigmy palms that stood between them and the next table. Leaning forward as she sat, she slid her cup of tea across the table to her new position.

"I'm not used to the sun. Under the dome, light's constant. Out here, it burns."

Jonas nodded, knowingly. "It's the little things, isn't it?"

Lindy situated herself so that she could comfortably face Jonas. "I don't know why it doesn't work. Are you sure that the probe was built to specs? It passed all of the tests?"

Jonas replaced his glasses, adjusted them up on his nose, added two teaspoons of sugar to his coffee and began to stir, flinching at the thought of it. "Yes. We've worked out all of the bugs. It passes all tests."

He pulled a cigarette from his pack and offered one to Lindy, who refused, lit it, took a long drag and blew the smoke out of the corner of his mouth, away from their table. "You used to smoke."

"Not allowed inside the dome. I'd been wanting to give it up."

"Good for you. I'll probably die smoking."

Lindy smiled. "Don't know about that. But you'll probably die because of it."

"I'm going to die of something. Might as well be what I enjoy. OK. Everything is exactly the same, except that our probe doesn't work. Why?"

"Jordan changed something, last minute."

"Changed…, what?"

"I don't know. He was logged into the database when I came over to wish him luck. Whatever he did caused an Error Code 317. And then I had to leave."

"Who else would know?"

"That would be Anthony Swincer. I'm already working on it."

"Well, Lindy," Jonas took a sip of coffee. "They're leaning very heavily on me to figure it all out. I've done my part. I've built the replica and it works to the specs you've provided. Yet, it's our problem. So, all I can say is, we're not leaving here until we have a plan. Is there any way you can get back into the dome?"

"No."

"So sure?"

"You have to think the code while looking into the scanner. The computer confirms that the person thinking the code is the same one that's looking in the scanner. Even if I had someone else's eye, the computer would know that it was me inputting the code. And even if I did get in, all of the alarms are going to go off and the place will be in instant lockdown until they find me."

"How did your cover get blown?"

"I accessed a secure link and was attempting to get information. I think the server recognized that there were too many users accessing the file and sent an alarm. That must've been what Anthony saw."

"Wasn't there a better way to get that information?"

"There wasn't time."

"So, what did you actually see?"

"On every previous run the probe always sounded like it wasn't tuned right. Jordan and Anthony were experimenting with different frequency combinations. The last run was smooth right up through my hearing range. It launched in a flash of light, just like what they thought would happen. We lost power and were left sitting in the dark. When back-up power came on, the probe was gone."

"You don't know if he got back?"

"No."

"Now..., what?"

"Jordan may not be coming back. I made a change in the program that if the test succeeded, the return coordinates would change."

Jonas took another long drag off of his cigarette, studying Lindy. "Why would you do that?"

"A couple of reasons."

"You might have compromised the entire project."

"Or saved it. If Jordan was successful, they would have the advantage. This way, it might still be a level playing field."

"That's pretty brutal. So, he might be out there, forever?"

"Forever, such a harsh word. If he's in a position to look at the program, he could figure it out."

"In case he doesn't, how do we get our hands on, what's his name, Anthony?"

"Like I said. I'm working on it."

Jonas squashed his cigarette out in the ashtray. "Remind me to never turn my back on you."

Tess tossed the pamphlet onto the table and then directed her gaze toward Ramon, who was busy emptying the contents from his latest task, house cleaning, into the trash.

"Ramon."

"Yes, Miss Tess."

"When you're done there, come over here. I want to talk."

Ramon closed the lid on the waste can and then joined her at the table.

"When those agents were here, how did you do that?"

"Do what, Miss Tess?"

"Telepathy."

"That's part of Code two, Miss Tess."

"It's not mentioned here in the manual."

"That manual? Yes. That is correct. That model does not have that feature."

"It's not even listed as one of the options."

"That would be true. I've read that information. It is not an option for any of those models."

"Yet, you look like one of those models. What model are you?"

"I am a 3DX – 5JB."

"It's not listed here."

"That would be correct. I am built to look like those models, but I am not any of those models."

"Then, why was I given this pamphlet when I purchased you?"

"To avoid suspicion, Miss Tess."

"Suspicion? Why would anyone be suspicious of me buying a robot? Half the population owns one kind of a robot or another."

"Miss Tess, the time has come for us to have this conversation. I have been programmed to reveal certain facts as the need arises. It is for your own safety that you are on a learn as you go basis."

"What? Ramon, you're a robot. I am the owner. You do as I say."

"That is correct, Miss Tess."

"What conversation?"

"Your order for me to go to Code Two launched a secondary program that instructs me to have additional duties, one of which is to maintain communications with you. Normally, all that means is that I watch your actions and search for ways to be of assistance. If, in Code Two, I detect danger, as with that male visitor carrying a loaded weapon, my instructions are to communicate pertinent information by any means possible."

"So..., telepathy? How was that possible?"

"I have been programmed to have curiosity. One of my greatest concerns is why you do what you do. So I compare your moods and words to your brainwaves and have learned what information is stored where and how you use it. I have, in the process, learned your own private language. And I have the ability to transmit my concerns to your brain."

"You know how I *think*?"

"Yes," Miss Tess. "Conceptually."

"Why is it that I have you and not the model that I thought I was buying?"

"I am that basic model, with modifications."

"By whom?"

"Jordan Blake."

"When did that happen?"

"One hundred and twenty-three days before his departure. Jordan asked if he could make some modifications and you replied that it was OK as long as I could still cook. Laughter from both of you."

"What other modifications?"

"My memory and processing speed have been greatly increased. I have access to all publicly available information. I have some mechanisms that will aid in your defense...,"

"Such as?"

"The male had the RX700 Phasor. I have no defense for that, but I have the ability to transmit a sound that would temporarily disable his ability to use it."

"I see. And would it disable everybody else as well?"

"No, Miss Tess. It is a frequency particular to each human."

"Would that cause permanent damage?"

"A short burst would act like a stun gun, without the electricity. A longer burst would knock him down. A continued burst would eventually kill him."

"This is also from Jordan's modification?"

"Yes, Miss Tess."

"What is Code Three?"

"I am not authorized to divulge that information at this time."

"I command it."

"I am sorry, Miss Tess. Denied."

"Go to Code Three."

"I am sorry, Miss Tess. Denied. Certain conditions have to exist before I am allowed to go to Code Three."

"More of Jordan's modifications?"

"Yes, Miss Tess."

"What if I don't want you to have these features? What if I just want a plain, old robot?"

"That would not be wise, Miss Tess."

"I will decide what's wise." Tess shuffled through the receipts and pamphlets concerning Ramon. "Why would it not be wise?"

"Because then you would be in grave danger."

"Why?"

"My curiosity programming allows me the freedom of predicting odds of future events. If Jordan's testing at work is successful, visitors will come asking. Predicted."

"What do you know of Jordan's work?"

"Miss Tess. I studied him the entire time he lived here, after the modifications. He spent much time thinking about his work."

"What did he think about me?"

"He has strong feelings for you."

"Why did he leave?"

"I predicted that he would leave, but got the date wrong. Jordan had two lines of income, Cond-Orbit and a coded account. I started noticing that his thoughts associated with the coded account increased with time. This was a source of increasing stress for him. He had to resolve it."

"So..., why am I in danger?"

"Because of your relationship with Jordan. I predict that more questions from the government will follow, that the encounters could turn violent, your last visitors were armed, and that there are four parties, at least, that are now interested in Jordan's work."

"Four?"

"You, Cond-Orbit, the U.S. Government, and Lindy Moore."

"How do you know about Lindy?"

"It was recently posted on Cond-Orbit internal mail. A security alert."

"That's a confidential line."

"Yes, Miss Tess."

"How did you...? Never mind. So, you predict that we are going to hear from Lindy Moore?"

"Or, one of her associates. And I predict that it will happen within the next seventy-two hours."

"And you've determined that this encounter will be dangerous?"

"That is always a possibility, Miss Tess."

Catfish

The message title was, "Great work, Anthony."

Normally, Anthony would not open anonymous mail, but this one was apparently complimenting him for something that he had done.

Anthony figured that he did many great things and that too many of them had gone unnoticed. He opened the mail from someone called Catfish:

Anthony,

Just wanted to say that we have been closely following your work and believe that much of the forward progress has been due to your diligence in interpreting the theories and helping to formulate the equations that have helped put this project on the road to success.

As a token of our appreciation, we have deposited five thousand IM's into your account. There is no action on your part that is, or will be, required. It is simply an expression of thanks.

Sincerely,

Catfish

Anthony sat back in his chair and allowed himself another sip of soda.

Five thousand IM's! Who is this?

He brought up his finance page and checked the balance in his account. There it was, five thousand additional IM's.

He retrieved his soda and took another long sip. He'd been meaning to cut down. The doctor had warned him that his sugar intake was far too high and that he was heading for diabetes. But the sugar-free stuff was crap. It tasted metallic to his tongue and if he didn't like the taste of something, he was done with it.

A little bit of sugar is better than a lot of crap. I'll make the sacrifice and just drink more water. I just hope that this water won't make me sick.

It was better to live inside a dome. Yes, expenses were higher. But the quality of living was better. The air was filtered, constant and clean, same as the water. Tap water under the dome tasted better than filtered water outside. Security was better. Winners lived inside a dome.

Five thousand IM's! Security deposit and two month's rent. I could be out of here before the weekend's over. Two trips. I could move in two trips.

He read the message again.

What if it's a trap? Hmm. They're not asking for anything.

Thumping his fingers on his desk, Anthony wondered about a reply.

Sudden influx of money, working a secret job? Doesn't look good. Still, they know who I am. They've recognized my work. They must be in the project, too. Otherwise, how would they know?

Anthony got up, went to the bathroom, visited the kitchen, got himself a hand full of mixed nuts and returned to the message. Then, he typed:

Dear Catfish,

Thank you for the recognition. I greatly appreciate the praise. But I cannot accept this money. How do I return it?

Sincerely,

Anthony

He spent the next hour getting dinner. Normally, he would eat much earlier. But he was making progress on Error Code 317 and wanted to finish working out the equations. After dinner, he returned to his mail and discovered that Catfish had replied.

Anthony,

We are sorry, but there is no way to return the money. It came from a slush fund that is used to quietly reward certain individuals for their extra special efforts. You fall into that category.

Thanks again,

Catfish

Tess was sick of the news. The air coming across the Pacific was intolerable. It wasn't fair, getting someone else's bad air. People were starving everywhere, riots and fighting taking place around the world, food shortages, and *still* no one was talking about controlling populations or weapons. The planet was in a tailspin and no one seemed to care.

The scourge of the Earth, humans! The good politicians don't get elected and the bad ones have corporate backing.

Gotta make sure the laws favor business. Keep that economy going. Keep up the corporate profits. Screw quality of life. They're living inside domes. Lucky for them.

Tess turned off the news and sat in the silence, frowning. "Ramon?

"Yes, Miss Tess?"

"What else does Code Two do?"

"A secondary set of processors become available, Miss Tess. Translations of every known form of communication will be provided from me to you in real time, by telepathy if necessary, and my communications link speed to the known world is increased a thousand fold. I am authorized to take defensive maneuvers to save your life."

"The sound thing, right?"

"Correct, Miss Tess. I also have the ability to disable any electronic devices in the immediate area."

"How do you do that?"

"I scan all signaling surrounding you, analyze, and if there appears to be danger to you, neutralize that signaling."

"All of this from Jordan?"

"Yes, Miss Tess."

"Why? What has Jordan gotten himself into? And why am I part of it?"

"I cannot understand the illogical reasons why most humans do what they do. I have curiosity, but I cannot understand passion, which is what drives Jordan. He has detected a force that is destructive to his current work, which is his passion, and he wants to be rid of it."

"Why am I involved?"

"You are also a part of his passion. He wants to protect that."

"He has no right to include me, not without my consent."

"That is correct, Miss Tess."

"What if I don't share his passions?"

"That would be incorrect, Miss Tess. You share his passions, even though you don't allow yourself to admit it."

"What? I have passion about many things."

"That is true, Miss Tess. But the passion that you have for these things without Jordan is greatly diminished."

"How can you know that? You're just a robot."

"That would be incorrect, Miss Tess. I am not just a robot. I am your robot, programmed to keep you safe and happy. To do that most effectively, it is imperative that I know how you think. Therefore...,"

"I don't like that. I don't want you spying on my every thought. I order you to stop. Stay out of my head."

"You are advising that portion of my programming to shut down, Miss Tess?"

"Yes."

"It is a default setting to the ON position. I must warn you that without the ability to monitor your thoughts, you will also lose the ability to communicate with me by telepathy."

"Good."

"I must warn you that my ability to be of assistance in an emergency will be greatly diminished. I recommend that I be allowed to automatically go to Code Two in the event that you have visitors."

"Denied. I will determine what happens and when."

"Yes, Miss Tess."

"Is that program shut down?"

"It is done."

"Good."

Vacancy

"Anthony Swincer?"

"Speaking."

"I'm sorry to keep you waiting, but the list for applicants wanting to live under any of the domes in your preferred areas is three months long, at least."

"Three months?"

"Correct. The wait could be longer. It depends on availability, new construction and the movement of people. But three months has been pretty much the norm for the last two years."

Anthony knew what that meant. More air pollution, drinking water getting not only salty, but also contaminated with chemicals, pesticides and radioactive contamination.

Harmless, they say. Yes, it could kill a rat if they drank enough. But humans would have to drink a hundred times what they normally drink for it to even be considered as potentially harmful. It's just that it stays in the water for a thousand years.

"Well, add my name to the list. Is there any way to make this whole process go faster?"

"You can get next available for five thousand IM's."

"Five thousand?"

"Or, for three thousand, we will put you in the expedite group. There, the waiting list is more like six weeks."

"Is this money applied toward the cleaning deposit and rent, once a place is available?"

"I'm afraid not."

"Who gets that money?"

"It's collected as a fee and is used to pay expenses, same as any business."

"The basic fee is a thousand. It costs two thousand

more to put my information on a different list?"

"Yes."

"And it costs an additional four thousand to put me on a preferred list? How long does it take to move me from one list to the other? Five seconds?"

"Mr. Swincer, do you want on the list, or not?"

"Yes," Anthony sighed. "Put me on the three month list."

"Right. Let's see, I'll need some information and...,"

"And..., what?"

"Something just came in. But it's in a very limited area."

"Where?"

"Well, probably not."

"Where?"

"It's under a company dome. You'd have to work for that company."

"What company?"

"Let's see..., still looking. Oh, here it is. Cond-Orbit. A place just became available."

"I work for Cond-Orbit!"

"It says you have to have a security clearance. Do you have that?"

Anthony felt his pulse quicken.

This is almost too good to be true! No commute to work! Live right there on premises. Yes, yes, yes!

He cleared his throat. "Yes, I do. How much is it?"

"A thousand IM's a month. They're willing to waive the seven hundred IM cleaning deposit if you take it, as is."

"So, three thousand total, first and last months rent, and your fee of one thousand?"

"Yes. Would you like to look at the place first?"

And take a chance that someone else might grab it, sight unseen?

"No. I'll take it, as is. How do I transfer the money?"

48

"I am sending you our account number as we speak. You transfer the funds and reference it to the attached number. When the transfer takes place, we will send you the address and code for entry. Meanwhile, I'll put a hold on the place."

"How long will the transaction take?"

"Usually within the first three business days after we verify your funds. Anything else I can do for you?"

"So, if I transfer funds right now and you see that transfer, will the transaction take place today?"

"It depends on when it's processed."

"That's a different department?"

"Yes."

"I'm sending the money now. Do you know how to verify funds?"

"Of course, I do. But I don't work in that department."

"I see. But you could make the transaction if you did?"

"Yes."

"I've just sent three thousand and fifty IM's. That extra fifty is for whoever processes the agreement. Thank you."

"Thank you, Mr. Swincer."

Anthony broke off the connection feeling pretty good, excellent, in fact.

How lucky is that?

Got myself a place inside the dome.

Woo hoo!!

Sometime after midnight, a mass of hot air began to form just under the top of the dome, swirling within itself, columns of highly charged particles.

If anyone had been looking, they would have seen, with the moonlight shining through, what looked like an endless stream of flying insects, following the leader on a high energy jaunt across the massive confines of the dome.

Zodi had been called out because one of the communications towers had failed. She parked her vehicle next to the front door of the site, got out, and plugged the vehicle's charge cord into the outlet.

Running a little low. Gotta make my rounds today. Don't want to get stuck.

She walked around the truck, grabbing her tools and meter along the way, and then headed for the front door. The scanner recognized her and de-energized the lock. Three dead bolts slid back into their chambers, the door opened and the lights came on.

The power pack for the transmitter was burned up. Knowing that she did not have a spare, and finding none on site, she called Adan, who always kept spares in his vehicle.

"Hello?"

"Adan. This is Zodi."

"Zodi? What..., what time is it?"

"Um..., three twenty-eight. I need a favor."

"Three twenty-eight?" He yawned. "This better be good."

"I need a power pack for a Multi-Wave Five Hundred."

"At three-thirty in the morning? Zodi, go get some sleep."

"Can't. I got a call-out. They want this antenna up and running yesterday. It's one of the main links."

"Where are you?"

"Station six."

"Oh," another yawn. "OK. I'll be there as soon as I can. But you owe me. I told you to keep spares with you."

"Carrying all that stuff, that little car hardly moves."

"And now it's making me move. I'll be there in about a half."

"Thanks, Adan. Hey! Can you bring me a coffee and roll on your way?"

"Well, now you're just pushing it."

"Thanks, Adan. I'll get the old pack out so all we have to do is slide the new one in place."

"We? Oh. Now I'm doing your work, too?"

Zodi laughed. "Well, yeah. That's why you're paid the big bucks."

"I'm paid the same as you. Bye, Zodi."

An hour later, they powered up the new unit, made sure it was working and then headed for the door.

Outside, standing next to their vehicles, they were finishing the last of their coffee when a black, shadow passed across Adan's face.

Zodi looked up, thinking that for a cloud to move that fast, there must be a storm going on outside the dome.

"What is that?"

The words were barely out of her mouth when a bright flash crackled loudly between the antenna and cloud.

Adan headed for the car door. "Get in!" He fell in behind the steering wheel and operated all of the windows to the up position.

Zodi jumped in the other side and slammed the door shut. "What *is* that?"

51

"No idea. Thought it was bugs or something until lightning came out of it."

"Are we safe in here?"

"I think. We've got four rubber tires beneath us."

"Let's go. Back up. I'll get my truck later."

"No. Wait. What's it doing?"

Leaning out over the dashboard, peering up through the windshield, they saw another flash of light snake between the cloud and tower, followed by a loud boom. The charge found its way down the wave-guide and into the building. A burst of light flashed out from beneath the door.

Adan groaned. "There goes the power pack."

Zodi nodded. "Whatever it is, it's in here, in the dome with us."

And then, as if somehow detecting that the exchange was dangerous, the thing, whatever it was, faded back into the night.

First Hint

Joseph was hunched over the desk studying the alarm layout on the monitor when the door opened. Glancing up, squinting into the light, he recognized Pierce and motioned him over.

"I can break down the exact time of any alarm, show corresponding video of the area, tell you what type of alarm and which system it came from. System A is the older, more expensive system. System B is the cheaper one that we just installed."

"OK. How do they compare?"

"The only way to enter this area without setting off an alarm is to input the code before opening any of the doors. We have assigned specific codes to all individuals so we know who is entering and when. Video surveillance is continuous."

"Sounds like you've got it all set up and under control. Yet, your call left doubts. What haven't you told me?"

"Last night we had another alarm, at two-sixteen. The motion sensor went off in System A. System B didn't pick up anything."

"Cameras pick up anything?"

"Not a thing."

"Odd."

"And then we got an alarm from the room next door, in the warehouse."

"What kind?"

"Motion. But none of the doors had been opened and, on video anyway, there was nothing moving inside. Both systems detected it."

"Well, Joseph. Sounds to me like you've got yourself a problem. Let me know when you've got it fixed."

"Do you have *any* ideas?"

"Lots of them. But I just got a call from Communications over on the east side. Seems they had some kind of problem at one of the antenna sites. The techs are saying that it was some kind of pulsating cloud. I have no idea what they're talking about but I guess I have to go over there and solve their problem."

"Maybe this is related."

"I hope so. Because then it becomes your problem."

"It doesn't make sense."

"I agree. So get on it and get me some answers. Are you going out there?"

"I guess I'd better. Maybe I should install a second alarm system in the warehouse."

"And then you'll get an alarm in staging and want to put an extra alarm in there. Sounds like you've got a more fundamental problem, like power to the entire alarm system is faulty. That's the only thing that could cause something like that."

"Unless these alarms are real. But I don't know of anything that could cause it."

"Me either."

"You're right. If both systems are having problems, it has to be power. I'll check into it."

"Get back to me when you find out something. Meanwhile, looks like we'll both be out of the office until sometime after lunch."

Dropping In

Anthony didn't like the sound of it. Somebody was at his front door. It was almost eleven, a time when he would normally be thinking about going to bed. But happily, this night was different. This night was for packing. As suspected, the paperwork was processed without sending it through the usual channels.

Figured that would work. Amazing what fifty IM's can do. Better than paying three thousand for first come, first serve. What a deal! I'll be moved in tomorrow.

The buzzer rang again. Whoever it was, they were persistent, that being the third ring. Normally, Anthony did not have visitors. Nobody wanted to converse with him because, talking with Anthony it was always about equations, theories, and numbers. Most people's eyes glazed over after a few minutes of conversation him. Most people, except the other engineers on the project, were just like him and he saw them every day anyway. Anthony quietly put his notes in the desk drawer and logged out of his computer.

Don't need anybody seeing what I do. Who is calling this late at night?

The record light blinked on.

"Anthony Swincer. My name is Vivian Bustworthy. And with me is Drake Walker. With are with the U. S. Government, Special Operations, and we'd like to have a moment of your time, if you don't mind."

What? What would they want with me?

"We would like to ask a few questions about your work with Jordan Blake."

Anthony leaned back in his chair.

Not authorized. I can't talk about my work with any-one outside my immediate department.

Good. I didn't want to talk with them anyway. Be-sides, it's too late for house calls.

You want to talk to me? Go through the channels at work. That's what they're for.

"I am going to leave a number that you can use to call us. It is imperative that you contact us at the earliest opportunity."

Right. That's what I want to do, talk to the govern-ment.

Anthony watched them leave and then, through the blinds, watched them stand near the street and continue their discussion. When he was sure they had gone, he finished packing and then went to bed.

The next morning, as he was bringing his stuff out-side, while getting everything ready for the move and just as he was setting his suitcase down, a hand reached around from behind and held a cloth over his mouth and nose.

The smell of ether flooded his senses. He strug-gled to turn around, to break free. He jammed his elbow into somebody's ribs and heard them curse, but they did not let go. Suddenly the world was spin-ning, a slow, winding motion all the way down to the ground.

Priorities

Malcolm opened the door and motioned for Tess to enter. This was a small room compared to other testing areas, about thirty feet wide and, stretching it, maybe fifty feet long. The walls and ceiling, she was told, were reinforced concrete, four layers thick while the probe stand, positioned in the middle of the room, was composed of some type of non-metallic tubing that was used to secure the probe and to provide links for the various hoses, electrical cables and whatever else was needed to make it all happen.

"So, this is it, huh?"

Malcolm nodded. "I get nervous every time I come in here. Not sure if, or when, Jordan will try to bring it back."

"Yet, it has no propulsion."

"Amazing, isn't it?"

"So, a song and a prayer was pretty much it."

"It speaks to Jordan's boldness in wanting to move ahead. He put the probe into manual control and took it full power. Why, we don't know."

"So, if it's still here, it just looks like empty space. Have you run some kind of test to see if anything is different between where we're standing and where the probe is supposed to be?"

"We've run every kind of test. That reality, world, whatever you want to call it, does not interact with this one."

"And you think telepathy can transcend these two realities? That's a pretty bold leap, Malcolm."

"That was Jordan's idea. I went along with it just to humor him. You know how he is. The concept was good. It wasn't going to cost much and it looked like he was going to get it to work. Like I said, this department leaps toward the conceptual."

Tess slowly walked around the stand, touching it here and there, amazed that something this complicated could actually *do* anything. One of the things that she liked about working for Cond-Orbit was that everything was new technology, trial and error and moving forward as fast as imagination, production and permits would allow.

And in the middle of all that, having worked with, having lived with Jordan, it had never occurred to her that one day he might be gone permanently. Yes, there was Lindy. Yes, he was into adventure. And yes, he loved intrigue. But all of that aside, Tess thought that the spark between them was special. There would always be some kind of connection over the years, maybe not quite what she wanted.

Ramon was right. I have more passion when I'm with him and I don't allow myself to admit it. I'll put Ramon back into Code Two. It's for my own good. You're getting too proud, girl, thinking you can boss a robot around.

Why did Jordan take the trouble to build Ramon if he didn't love me?

"Malcolm?"

"Yes."

"What happens behind all of those windows?"

"There is a team of technicians that monitor the input data over there," said Malcolm, pointing to the window on his left. "Directly across the room from them is another team that monitors the mechanical and electrical functions. The area behind me is for the techs that monitor the whole operation, cameras, alarms and the main console."

"How about that window over there?"

"For Anthony. He and his team oversee the operation and are paid to come up with new ideas and punch holes in the old ones, if any exist."

"Well, apparently one does."

"We haven't lost Eclipse. We just haven't found it yet."

"It? Him. You've lost Jordan."

"In all fairness, we think he lost himself. He wasn't supposed to go to full power. We are not nearly ready for that yet. All he was supposed to do on this trial was monitor life support."

"How about Lindy? What about her?"

"She's disappeared as completely as Jordan. We know that she is not under any of the domes in the immediate area. She'd have to go through Security and she can't do that. We know she hasn't left the country."

"OK, Malcolm. You bring me here, show me where it all happened, and give me a bit more information. How are my thoughts, even if they are put into a thousand different packets of information, going to reach him? If you can't communicate with the craft that was designed for that purpose, what chance do I have?"

"Are you giving up?"

"No. But I just don't see...,"

"We've never moved ahead by thinking that something was impossible. This is your opportunity to be on the cutting edge of technology. Right now you are part of a team of very skilled scientists, all of them dedicating their entire lives to this kind of exploration. You're smart, intuitive...,"

"Quit buttering me up. Don't worry, Malcolm. I'm not giving up."

Seriously

"Ramon, I authorize you to go back to Code Two."

"Miss Tess. I am pleased to see that you have come to your senses."

"Pleased to see? You're a robot. How can you be pleased to see anything?"

"It is a phrase used by Jordan when the results worked out as he hoped. It is programmed into one of my 'commonly used phrases' index."

"And, come to your senses?"

"Programmed by Jordan to mean, when logic prevails."

"So, according to both you and Jordan, it is logical for me to keep you in Code Two, now that I've discovered what it is."

"That is correct, Miss Tess."

"What else can you tell me?"

"Now that I've been authorized to resume Code Two, I am currently updating all relevant data. One item has just been brought to my attention, Anthony Swincer did not report for work today even though it's a Sunday. He has not missed a day of work since he has been hired and that has been one thousand nine hundred and forty-seven days."

"Anthony. The man who works for Cond-Orbit?"

"That is correct."

"You seem to have some sort of authorized connection into Cond-Orbit's private matters. Is that correct?"

"Yes, Miss Tess, authorized by Jordan Blake."

"Jordan has trusted you with an awful lot of information. If captured, are you a security risk?"

'No, Miss Tess. If I am about to be neutralized, the last thing I do is to self-destruct. I will burn up all traces of information, including myself."

"Does that bother you?"

"Does what bother me?"

"Knowing that you will cease to exist."

"I am a tool for your safety and convenience, Miss Tess. I, as you know it, do not exist. I is merely a name given to me by Jordan that refers to the programs that are running to make those things happen."

"OK, Ramon..., what's next?"

"I have just discovered that Anthony Swincer rented a condo inside Cond-Orbit but that he has not yet moved in. I have also updated the status of Cond-Orbit's Eclipse Project. Jordan is still missing. He has not posted to our private site for three days. Lindy Moore's whereabouts is still a mystery. My curiosity programming is engaged in the odd coincidence of both her and Anthony missing at the same time. And my curiosity programming is also predicting that Lindy Moore might be interested in you."

"Why me?"

"Lindy Moore left the dome before testing ended, according to dome access records. This leads me to presume that she does not know Jordan's current status. She may think that Jordan is here, or that you would know of his whereabouts, or the results of the testing."

"You know about the testing?"

"Yes, Miss Tess."

"You're a moving security violation."

"If anyone attempts to take this information, I have been programmed to...,"

"I know. We just went through that."

"Depending on the circumstances, Miss Tess, I can also feed false information. It is impossible for any unauthorized person to gain this information."

"And those authorized parties are...?"

"Jordan Blake."

"What about me? I own you."

"You are the only other authorized party, up to Code Two."

"Why not Code Three?"

"We have already had this conversation, Miss Tess. Certain conditions have to exist before...,"

"I know, before you're allowed to go to Code Three."

"That is correct. But when you do, should you survive, you will have complete access to all of my facilities."

"Should I *survive*?"

"Miss Tess, I predict that you will be going where no woman, or man, except perhaps Jordan Blake, has gone before. I predict that you will travel beyond humankind's knowledge. There is some element of danger to that."

"Me? Ha! I don't think so. I'm not going anywhere. Jordan did this to himself. I'm not risking my life for his folly."

"Yes, Miss Tess."

Friendly Chat

Anthony Swincer awoke to the sound of Mozart's Serenade No. Ten for Thirteen Wind Instruments in B Flat while a misty spray fell down through shafts of red, green, and golden light into the orchid garden below.

Anthony was not a plant person or an animal person. In fact, Anthony was not even an outdoor person. He greatly preferred the glare of a computer screen, surrounded by darkness or, just the opposite, the bright artificial lights of the testing area, anything not natural.

Yet, here was something truly beautiful. Listening to the music, playing softly from somewhere out of view, watching the mist falling through the light, scarce here, thicker over there, airy waves of colored droplets drifting downward through the soft light.

There must be a formula for that. How much mist passes by in any given second? Wave after wave. Why doesn't it pass uniformly? What's the equation for that? Wait. Where am I?

Rolling over to his other side, Anthony quietly took in the room. Opposite the orchid garden was a conveniently located workstation, big screens, lots of desk space and, next to that, a small kitchenette, fresh fruit on the counter, refrigerator humming quietly.

Sitting up, looking over the foot of his bed, some sort of table and seating area, what looked like a bathroom, at least that's what Anthony hoped it was, and beyond that, a door.

Getting up, Anthony found his clothes, ID, all of his personal things, including his luggage, which had been stored inside a small closet. On the kitchen counter was a dish of Danish, his favorite kind, a freshly brewed pot of coffee, breakfast cereals, everything he could possibly want, and all at his fingertips. He smiled.

If I've been abducted, it's not too bad..., yet. Where am I?

A knock on the door. Glancing toward the sound, Anthony noticed that the door was unlocked. "Wait a minute." He quickly pulled on his pants, put on a shirt and checked his hair in the mirror. "Come in."

Lindy entered the room, looking good, smiling. "Hi Anthony."

"Lindy Moore? I should've known."

"Did you have a good rest?"

"Where am I?"

"Everything satisfactory as far as your room goes?"

"From what I've seen, yes. Where am I? Why am I here?"

"Anthony, patience is a virtue."

"I've been abducted! You have no right to...,"

"Abducted? Yes. But not in a bad way. Not when you hear what I have to say."

"Whatever it is that you want to call it, I am not where I want to be. I insist that I be released immediately."

"Tony, Tony, Tony. I am disappointed. You, of all people. What I've always admired about you is your refusal to stay within the boundaries. I can't count how many times you have saved the project from yet another of their many foolhardy mistakes. You can do with numbers and equations what most people can't do, even with the help of their computers. I would think that you, of all people, would be interested in what the proposition is."

"After that, I'm free to go?"

"Yes."

Anthony stood there for a minute, judging her sincerity. Then he went to the coffee maker, poured a cup and offered it to her.

OK, Anthony. Keep sharp. She's the enemy now, even though she's never treated me badly.

This will be interesting. What will she offer?

Lindy accepted it with a smile. "Good." She took the cup, found a cheese Danish on the plate, placed it on a napkin and then headed for the table. Anthony poured himself a cup, placed two glazed donuts on a napkin and seated himself across the table from her.

"Let's hear it."

"Who do you think is going to get all of the credit for the project?"

"Cond-Orbit, of course. They're funding it."

Lindy smiled. "No. They are not funding it. And I can prove it."

"Then..., who is?"

"A conglomerate of several interested parties, not from the US."

"OK. Say I believe that. So, what?"

"They're going to own all of the patents. If this project is successful, and it's going to be, the financial gain is almost beyond comprehension. What percentage of that are you going to get?"

'None. I'm a paid consultant."

"And yet you've provided the innovative thinking that made many of these ideas successful."

"That's what I'm being paid to do."

"Your name won't even appear. You will have little, if any, publicity. It will read something like, "Cond-Orbit, with lead engineer, Jordan Blake and team, discovered..., whatever. Anthony, where are you in this picture?"

"They're paying me very well."

"They're paying you nothing compared to what they're going to get. Do they offer a nice little retirement after twenty years? No. They don't, because you're a contractor. You'll have to do your own retirement."

"OK. Say I buy that. Get to the point."

"What if I offer you a fully equipped lab, a team of trained professionals, you'll have heard of many of them, all of the latest designs on the probe and all of the programs that run it?"

"With me running the show?"

"Yes. It would read, "Anthony Swincer and team...," and you would get acknowledgement for your ideas, part of the royalties from the patents, and we'd start off by doubling your salary. From there, the sky's the limit, literally."

"It won't work. It would take at least five years to catch up, even if you already had a probe. There are so many design changes that...,"

"We have a probe."

Anthony put his cup down, carefully, until it clinked onto the plate. And then he took a large bite of the second donut and chewed for a long time. "You have a probe?"

Lindy smiled. "I thought that might get your attention."

"How far along is it?"

"Exactly the same as the one inside Cond-Orbit."

"Exactly? Like what Jordan flew?"

"Flew?"

"You know what I mean. Tested. Launched. Energized. Projected from. There isn't really a word for it yet, is there?"

Lindy smiled, sipping her coffee. "No, there isn't. And yes, it's exactly the same."

"It works?"

"Absolutely, except for that last run. Something was different about that last run. What changes were made?"

Anthony answered with a shrug and a tight smile. "You know I can't answer that."

"The final adjustment. Jordan did it. I saw him at the computer just before the launch. I came over to wish him luck. I couldn't see what he was doing, so I don't know. But if anyone does, I'm guessing it's you. That's my offer, Anthony. We need you."

"I can't just leave Cond-Orbit. I have integrity. My name is on this, even if I'm not given credit."

"I'm not asking you to leave Cond-Orbit. I'm asking you to work for us, as well."

"It's Top Secret, Lindy. I shouldn't even be talking to you."

"Of course, they're calling it Top Secret. Anyone can come up with a stamp. They're not the government. I've got a whole wall full of Top Secret papers, manuals, books, back in my office. How many are authentic? How many have been distributed as Top Secret, but are secretly false information? It's a game."

"I'm afraid I can't accept your offer. It may all be a game, but I'm just one of the pawns."

Lindy smiled. "You have a chance to be the King."

"No, thanks. How do I get out of here?"

"We have a transport that will escort you back to your house. You will be blindfolded, of course. I am sorry. Security, and all of that. I noticed that you were packed. You were leaving?"

"I'm moving inside Cond-Orbit."

"Oh. That would be my old flat."

"Yours?"

"Of course. No places ever open up inside and I had to leave in a hurry, didn't I? They want to keep collecting that rent money."

"Cond-Orbit? I don't think they're worried about rent money."

"Cond-Orbit doesn't run the day to day business inside the dome. It's contracted out. If they don't collect rent, they lose money. You'll like it, large bedroom, cute, little kitchenette and well-equipped office. Oh. The place comes with a robot. Her name is Adelle. I'll give you the code so you can re-program her. Tell Jordan I said, "Hi.""

"I would, if I could. He never...," Anthony stopped.

Can't say that! Damn you, Anthony! Suckered you, right in.

"Oh?" Lindy looked horrified. "Poor Jordan! He didn't make it?"

Anthony stood to shake her hand. "Lindy, best of luck to you and your project. I've said enough. Can a transport be ready for me in five minutes?"

Lindy rose and extended her hand. "I'll let them know. Thank you, Anthony, for your time. I am sorry that it had to be under these circumstances. I was going to make you the offer earlier, but as you know, I had to leave in a hurry. If you change your mind...,"

"I won't."

She handed him his LifeLink. "This is yours. I've sent you my contact info in case you do." She turned to go, hesitated. "Oh, I'll send you the code to program Adelle. She's a good housekeeper and she knows how to cook. Give her your favorite recipes. Best of luck to you."

"Thank you."

Closing the door behind her, Lindy turned right, walked down the hallway, pushed the elevator button to take her up to ground level.

Once outside, she walked down a dirt and weed path, watching out for snakes, lizards, whatever else might be living in the area, and when she reached the western ridge, found a rock to sit on while she placed a call to Adelle.

"Yes, Miss Lindy?"

"Anthony Swincer will be arriving. Allow him to program you to Head of Household."

"It will be allowed."

"And then there are a few other things I'd like for you to do."

"Yes, Miss Lindy?"

Joseph waited for the gate to slide open and then hurried to catch up to Pierce, who was already heading for one of the two person transports that would take them back to HQ.

There were transports for two, four, eight, and sixteen people with some of the largest size transports also serving the construction personnel, having fold down seats to provide more room for their tools and equipment. All travel throughout dome, except for dome maintenance personnel, was accomplished with these transports.

Once an address was input, the central computer determined the course, speed and priority of the transport, which ones yielded right of way if two cars met at the same intersection at the same time. The only control for most passengers was an emergency stop button, unless you had a code that allowed additional instructions.

Pierce selected a two-person private, sat down at the controls, slid his card through and programmed in the address. Joseph entered the car, sat on the other side of the console, facing Pierce. He would be riding backwards.

"Can you assign me an expedite pass when we get back?" Joseph asked, fastening his safety harness. "I like how other cars have to stop for you."

"It's one of the few perks, Joseph. There aren't that many."

"But..., if I have to go back out to the antenna site...,"

"It's only going to save you five minutes. It'll take me an hour to get you upgraded. What do you think caused that outage?"

Joseph shrugged. "I believe the techs. They both told the same story. And they had two burned out power packs to prove it. Alarms didn't tell us anything. Every one of them went off. Problem is, what is it?"

Pierce rubbed his hands through his hair. "What it is. Where it is. Why it is. When is it going to happen again? And who's causing it? Those are my questions. I'm going to call a meeting when we get back. I want you to attend."

"Meeting? With whom?"

"Energy department. I want to know if they've been doing any testing, have changed out any equipment, or have experienced anything odd lately. Dome maintenance. I want to know if their routines are up to date and if they've had any kinds of problems. If I can't get a meeting going for this afternoon, it will be for tomorrow morning, first thing."

"That serious?"

"A cloud that spews lightning bolts. What do you think, Joseph? If it took out that antenna site that easily, it wouldn't be hard to take out a whole bunch of other stuff. What else is it capable of? Where is it right now? How come we can't see it? Is it in here with us? Or, is it coming and going through the dome walls? Do we have an unprotected opening somewhere? Yes, Joseph. It's serious "

"I wonder if it's related to the alarm problem that I'm having."

"Your problems are inside Cond-Orbit's manufacturing plant. This is the entire dome." Pierce retrieved a note pad from his pocket and noted that. "Hmm. I've heard rumors that they've had some kind of accident in there. You know anything about that, Joseph?"

"There is one section that is completely off-limits

to me and my entire crew. No access, period. I don't know what goes on in there."

"If it's affecting safety within the entire dome, it's my concern and they better tell me. Malcolm runs the show over there, right?"

"Yes."

"We'll invite him to this meeting, as well."

Malcolm thumped his fingers nervously on his desk, waiting for Stella to answer. The meeting had not gone well and Malcolm did not like to lie. Pierce had requested an emergency meeting. Malcolm had cringed at the thought of it.

Don't need a bunch of people asking questions. Got my own set of problems. Don't need his as well. Lightning inside the dome? Crimanently!

Stella picked up. "Hey, Malcolm. What's up?"

"I think we've got ourselves a problem."

"How's that?"

"The Director of Dome Operations, a guy named Pierce, roped me into a meeting this morning."

"I've met him."

"He says that a lightning cloud took out one of the communications towers on the east side of the dome."

"Lightning? Inside the dome?"

"That was my reaction, exactly."

"What does he think is causing it?"

"He doesn't know. He grilled the Dome Maintenance people. They claim the pressurization is normal and that all routines are up to date. And then he went after the Power Department, asking about old or replaced equipment."

"What did he ask you?"

"What was going on inside our plant. I told him the usual stuff, manufacturing parts for orbiting communities. When he asked about the probe testing area. I told him that that area was off-limits and that we are running a safe, reliable operation."

Stella laughed. "Well, that might hold him off for a little while. If there's another incident, I'd guess he'll be back with more questions. Do you think the probe is causing it?"

"I hope not," Malcolm sighed.

"What do you think is happening?"

"I'm guessing that Jordan is trying to return."

"But he's missing the target?"

"Something like that."

"Shouldn't that be in the program?"

"Of course. But if we can't communicate, we don't know. It may be impossible for him to come home."

"Pierce will insist on inspecting your area."

"He can't. Cond-Orbit owns the dome. Pierce just works for the company that maintains it. If the bigwigs upstairs want to expose their own secret project to public scrutiny, that's their decision. Mine is to protect the project and move it forward."

"Our side will have something to say in the matter as well. I'm going to run this up and get some decisions before it spins out of control."

"Good idea. I'll do the same."

"Maybe we should disassemble the whole project."

"And leave Jordan hanging?"

"At least until this blows over."

"I don't think it's going to blow over. Not until Jordan lands or blows himself up."

"He can't take us, and by that I mean all of you living inside the dome, with him when he goes, can he?"

"Stella, I don't even want to ask that question."

"By the way, I sent two of my people over to visit Anthony Swincer. They have not been able to contact him."

"He missed a day of work yesterday, first time ever. I stopped by the lab to see if he'd made any progress. Nobody had seen him."

"Not good. Give me a call when you know something?"

"Right. You'll do the same?"

"Got it. Bye, Malcolm. Good luck."

The place had a sunken living room with a 3D movie-sized screen at one end. There was a bookshelf along the adjacent wall with an aquarium built in. The side of the room opposite the big screen was comprised of two steps up to a small dining area, and beyond that, the kitchen. Adjacent to the dining area, Anthony discovered a study, and next to that, a half bath. Opposite the wall with the bookshelves were four steps leading up to the master bedroom, the only bedroom, and a full bath.

Anthony sat behind Adelle and accessed her control panel. He input the code that Lindy had given him and, when the green LED flashed, said, "Adelle, this is Anthony. I am your new master. You may call me Tony."

"Yes, Mr. Tony. Welcome to the flat. Shall I get you something to eat? A drink? How may I make you comfortable?"

"A glass of water with ice would be wonderful. I'm going to look around."

"Yes, Mr. Tony."

The place had been searched. Dresser drawers had been emptied and turned upside down. All furniture had been moved away from the walls, searched and the closet emptied. Lindy's clothes had been scattered everywhere. Books and papers were strewn across the floor.

Picking up her clothes, Anthony paused over her panties and bras and wondered what else she might have been persuaded to give up as part of the bargain. Yes, she had been Jordan's girlfriend, but he was as good as gone. And even if he did come back, those two would no longer be together.

Wouldn't mind shacking up with her for a while. That would make life interesting. Maybe I was a little too hasty with my decision. I'll box this stuff up and figure out a way to get it back to her. Hmmm.

Adelle returned with a glass. "Your water, Mr. Tony."

"Thank you."

"When you have a moment, Mr. Tony, please fill out the menu options at the main console. I have been programmed to cook anything that you see. The sooner that you inform me of your choices the more likely I will be able to prepare them on time. Grocery delivery inside the dome has a twenty-four hour lag time."

"So, if I want to eat something that you don't stock, I'll have to wait twenty-four hours for delivery of those items?"

"That is correct."

"What's in stock?"

"Which cultural foods do you prefer?"

"Italian."

"In the freezer, one twelve inch sausage-pepperoni pizza, one two-serve portion of lasagna...,"

"Wait. Mexican."

"In the freezer compartment, cheese or chicken en-chiladas, chili-cheese tamales, carne asada burrito, one remaining, and there are ingredients for tacos. That would take about twenty minutes to prepare."

"A carne asada burrito. Do we have chips and sal-sa?"

"Affirmative."

"Ingredients for a margarita?"

"Affirmative."

"I'll take the margarita, chips and salsa now, carne asada burrito when it's ready. And please say yes instead of affirmative."

"Yes, Mr. Tony. Salted rim?"

"What?"

"Did you want the rim of your glass salted, Mr. Tony?"

"Why..., yes. That would be a nice touch. I'll be in the study."

"Yes, Mr. Tony."

Anthony discovered that his password worked on the secure line into the Eclipse Project. That was another advantage while living under the dome. All lines were controlled, monitored and secured by Cond-Orbit personnel. He could work at home.

Home! What nice ring that word has! I am home inside the dome! Hooray! I'd better give Malcolm a call and see what's up.

Adelle returned with one bowl of chips and another with salsa. The margarita was made just how Anthony liked them."

"Thank you, Adelle. You and I are going to get along just fine."

"My pleasure, Mr. Tony."

Anthony smiled as he input Malcolm's number.

"Malcolm here."

"Malcolm, this is Anthony."

"Where have you been? We've been looking all over for you."

"I'm in my new place, inside the dome."

"The dome? This dome?"

"Right. Just settling in as we speak."

"I tried to contact you yesterday, surprised that I didn't find you at the lab."

"I got hung up," said Anthony, thinking of Lindy's underwear. "What's up?"

"It seems that we have some kind of cloud inside the dome with us. It took out an antenna site. Blew it up."

"When?"

"Last night."

"A…, cloud? Can you see it?"

"I haven't seen anything. The techs that witnessed it said it looked like a swarm of bugs. But they saw it around three in the morning and you know how moonlight reflects in the dome."

As they were talking, Anthony opened up his briefcase, pulled out some papers and spread them across his desk. "What's the plan, Malcolm?"

"I need for you to come in. We're going to do a trial run with Tess Altman."

"Jordan's old girlfriend?"

"Right. She'll be here around seven. See if you can make it by then."

"Seven, huh?" Anthony scribbled the time down on a piece of paper sitting on the desk. "In the test lab?"

"Right."

"OK. I'll be there."

"Thanks, Anthony. Welcome to the dome."

Adelle, standing beside him, placed his burrito on the desk, opened a fresh container of salsa and placed it beside his dinner. "Dinner is served, Mr. Tony. Is there anything else I can do for you?"

Anthony smiled. "Not a thing. Everything's perfect."

Coming Clean

Malcolm tried Tess' LifeLink for the umpteenth time. No answer. Tess was never late and if she was going to be, she'd call. It was a quarter of eight, forty-five minutes late. Not like Tess at all.

Finally, he decided to give Stella a call. Malcolm had a thing for her, at first. He knew that he was not her type, not with his out of shape body and loss of hair.

Stella herself was a little on the heavy side but she was "built for breeding" as one of the engineers said one day. Malcolm admonished the engineer on the spot but secretly agreed.

Stella didn't seem too concerned about any suitors. Her job paid well and she loved to spend her extra time outdoors, not something Malcolm could do very often since he lived under the dome. All of that aside, they did work well together.

"Hey Malcolm. What's up?"

"One of my employees is late, almost an hour now."

"And this concerns me..., how?"

"She's on the project."

"What do you want me to do?"

"Can you see if all routes heading west toward our dome are on time and that there aren't any abnormalities?"

"Oh. That's easy. From how far out?"

"Twenty miles."

"Hang on..., Angel?"

"Yes, Miss Stella."

"Check inter-dome transport status, all lines twenty miles west of Cond-Orbit heading toward the dome for the last two hours."

"Yes, Miss Stella."

Malcolm sighed. "I need one of those."

"Best secretary I've ever had."

"Miss Stella. All vehicles have been on time and there have been no abnormalities. Should I check other modes of operation?"

"Hey, Malcolm. Did you hear that?"

"Yes."

"Anything else I can do for you?"

"Can you send someone by her place if I give you the address?

"Sure. Who are we looking for?"

"Tess Altman. She lives at...,"

"Tess? I have the address right here. We just talked to her. She's disappeared?"

"I know it's only been an hour. But she is never late. And she would contact me if she was going to be. Something's wrong."

"Since we're on the subject, we haven't been able to contact Anthony Swincer"

"He's here. I just talked to him."

"He hasn't been home in the last twenty-four hours."

"He's just moved into the dome."

"What dome? Cond-Orbit?"

"Yeah."

"Oh. That explains it. OK, Malcolm. I'll send a couple of agents over to check on Tess. Anything new on your magical cloud?"

"Nothing. I'm waiting for the report from Dome Security, hoping that they find something that takes the pressure off of me. If it hits again..., well, I guess the phrase, stirring up a hornet's nest, applies. And I'm inside it."

"I hear you. Good luck, Malcolm."

Down the hall, sitting behind the glass in the testing area, Anthony was regretting some recent decisions.

Taking five thousand IM's. Should've reported it. Too late to do that? Being abducted. Should've reported that as soon as I was released. Too late to do that? This is not looking good. Hmm. What to tell Malcolm?

The door opened behind him. Anthony saw Malcolm's reflection in the glass and motioned for him to sit in the seat on his left. When he had situated himself, Anthony pointed to the monitor.

"This is a graph of the four inputs to the probe. Below that are the composite light signals that make up each input, what we were monitoring just before Jordan disappeared."

Anthony clicked to the next image. "Here is a table that I've developed that displays heat produced by each input. And here is the total heat produced, at any given moment by all of the inputs combined. Now, we can make this live..., watch this."

Anthony went to the next screen, which showed total heat temperature output and video of the probe in its last few seconds before departure.

"Temperature builds to its highest point right when he goes full power and then drops sharply just before he disappears. Jordan hit a point where the probe was disengaging from this reality." He paused the display. "Right..., there. Three seconds earlier, he hit a frequency that resonated itself right out of here and had enough energy to make the leap. Barriers break down and poof, a tunnel."

"That's what we expected. But what were the frequency changes?"

"I can work it backwards, find the relationship of heat to frequency and we can get pretty close. None of this explains why we don't have communications, though. I'd guess that if Eclipse can't communicate, it's free floating. Jordan has to home back into the stand. If he doesn't, it's gonna go boom, like that antenna tower. Where's Tess?"

"Waiting," said Malcolm, wringing his hands.

"You understand that this idea most likely won't work."

"What other options?"

"Malcolm, have you considered evacuating the dome?"

"What?"

"If you think about it, we don't know how much energy the probe has anymore. It's unstable. We don't know what's going to happen."

"Evacuate the dome? Anthony, you understand that this project is secret, right?"

"Of course, but...,"

"How would we keep it quiet?"

"I understand. But there could be a fairly violent explosion. People are going to get hurt."

"Just so you know, I've tried to get some direction from the folks upstairs. They say, keep it quiet, make it to go away. If I evacuate the dome, there's no way to keep this project quiet. And if I don't evacuate and people die, this whole thing's going to hang on me."

Anthony nodded, thinking of Lindy.

Not such a bad deal after all. Malcolm hangs for this one. I switch sides with the knowledge learned from all of this, get more money, fame, and rights to the patents. She has a probe. I'm clean here. I've already advised Malcolm to clear the dome.

"What do you need for me to do, Malcolm?"

"First, we need Tess. She said she's ready to test the memory system. You've got the transducer part of it. We'll take the signals, convert them, and let them ride with the inputs to the probe..., well, where the probe should be anyway, and we take it back up to full power. That's about as close as we're going to get to talking to another universe…,"

Watching Malcolm, Anthony leaned back in his chair and tapped his pencil on the desk.

Lindy has a probe. What to do? What to do?

Ramon

Ramon had predicted this possibility. There were too many hours of the day that Tess was gone, out of the house, out of range, vulnerable. Functioning under the programming of Code Two, he was authorized to maintain communications, but there was a limitation to his range of telepathy.

Over time, connecting into the city's camera network, he had learned Tess' paths of travel. He was not able to follow every step, but he knew how long it took to get from one camera to another.

She was taking too long. Normally, it would take ten minutes from when she entered the park and when she exited, certainly no longer than fifteen. From the camera that overlooked the park, he could then observe her as she walked toward the underground station that would take her to the dome.

All of the cars had cameras. Logging into the transit system's video, he could observe which car she was in and follow her all the way to the dome. After that, he could link into Cond-Orbit's security system and follow her most anywhere.

But she never came out of the park. After waiting thirty minutes, he placed a call to the police.

"May I help you?"

"I'd like to report a missing person."

"I see. How long has this person been missing?"

"Forty minutes."

"I'm sorry. Did you say minutes? Or hours?"

"Minutes. At her rate of travel, she should take only...,"

"You have to be missing at least twenty-four hours before we consider anyone missing."

"Twenty-four hours?"

"That is correct. Who is this? I notice that this call is not identified."

"I am Ramon. I am a robot programmed to...,"

"Minutes may seem like hours to you, but to humans, it's a very short time. Robots cannot initiate police action. Tell your owner that you have to be reprogrammed for protocol. Who is your owner?"

Having already predicted the outcome of that call, Ramon disconnected.

Cannot locate Tess, or report her absence without revealing this identity.

Cannot locate or communicate with Jordan.

East tower struck by lightning inside dome. No reported cause.

Lindy Moore still missing.

Anthony Swincer moves inside dome after suspicious disappearance.

Ramon was working on all of these things at once, and a million others, looking for solutions, making predictions and calculating the odds.

Judd followed Lindy into the room, closed the door and remained in front of it while Lindy approached the table, where she smiled and motioned for Tess to do the same. Coming together from opposite sides, she held out her hand.

"At last we meet. I'm Lindy Moore."

Tess pulled out a chair, sat, and motioned for Lindy to do the same. "So, now I have a face to put with the name."

"I, too. Jordan was very fond of you. He spoke of you often."

"I, on the other hand, had no clue. Life is full of little surprises."

"So it is. Tess, I would like to start out by informing you that I am not your enemy. I am your friend."

"Ha! I've been abducted! I'm being held against my will. Not allowed to make a call. You've got that robot over there blocking the door."

"At least let me explain. Jordan and I are working together, a team. We work for the U. S. Government. Cond-Orbit is owned by a foreign conglomerate that has interests detrimental to the U. S."

"What? What do you take me for? That is a great bunch of people that work at that company. They are dedicated...,"

"Of course they are. What better way to cover up a spy operation than using those same people as a front? What happened to Jordan was no accident."

"And yet it happened. Jordan is gone and you're on the outside of the dome. Where are we, Lindy? Let me ask you that."

"Tess, I'm trying to save Jordan. We don't have much time. He loves you very much and he wants to be with you. We need to talk. The probe is designed to keep Jordan alive for up to one hundred and seventy hours. We're coming up on four days and they don't know how to bring him back."

"And you can help, how?"

"We can bring him back."

"We? That's the problem, Lindy. I don't know who "we" is. I need to make a call."

"To whom? Malcolm? That's exactly what I'm trying to say. He is the unwitting front for a conglomerate out of the Ukraine that is trying to subvert the entire U. S. project. They wanted to prove that the theory worked..., and sacrificed Jordan."

"Why?"

"Cond-Orbit discovered Jordan's and my true identities. There is a control booth inside the test area that has the final say in everything. Malcolm is in charge of that room. To the risk of everyone inside the dome, he allowed the probe to go full power."

"The whole dome..., at risk? Right."

"I've just learned that there was a lightning strike, at least that's what they're calling it, inside the dome. Burned up an antenna site."

"When?"

"Last night. Cond-Orbit can't explain why. You know what this is all about, don't you? Jordan's trying to land."

"Lindy, what are you after? I've been abducted. That's all I know. Everything else is hearsay until I can come to my own conclusions. And that's not going to happen if I'm stuck in here, is it? What do you expect from me?"

"I was just going to ask a similar question. What does Malcolm expect from you?"

"I can't discuss that."

"And here we find ourselves in a dilemma, don't

we? Tell me, Tess, what would it take for you to co-operate?"

"I want to see legitimacy. I want to see your credentials. I want to see Cond-Orbit reports of the accident. I want the freedom to make calls. I want to come to my own conclusions."

Lindy smiled. "Consider it done. Judd, retrieve Tess' LifeLink."

"Yes, Miss Lindy."

"Make sure she has whatever she wants." Lindy smiled as she stood. "While you are coming to your conclusions, I would like for you to see our plan as well." She held out her hand. "Judd will assist you however he can. I'm sorry. I cannot allow you to leave, yet. When that time comes, we'll have a car waiting to take you to your destination."

Hesitantly, Tess shook her hand.

Confirmed

Vivian opened the door slowly and cautiously peeked inside. "Anybody home? Tess? Tess Altman. Are you here? This is Vivian Bustworthy and my associate, Drake Walker. We're coming in."

Drake quietly removed his gun from the holster. Vivian had insisted on going in first. He followed closely behind, peering over her shoulder. Ramon met them at the doorway.

"I must warn you. You are on private property without permission. Unless you can show some sort of authorization, I must ask you to leave."

"We're here on official business," Vivian replied. "We're investigating the sudden absence of Tess Altman. Can you help us with that?"

"What is it that you wish to know?"

"Is she here on these premises?"

"No."

"When is she expected back?"

"She is expected back already."

"When was the last time you saw her?"

"Are you asking when she left these premises?"

"Yes."

"Miss Vivian, finding Tess is both of our concerns. Yet, I must insist that I verify your employment with whatever department you claim to be from, before I divulge further information."

"You stupid robot," said Drake. "We'll just turn you off and take your memory."

"Shut up Drake," said Vivian, irritated with his demeanor. "This is an intelligent robot. Robot, what is your name?"

"I am Ramon."

"Ramon, how would you verify?"

"I require a coded ID card or a link to your company. I will verify through your company's computer."

"Are you capable of reading all information on my card?"

"That has not been determined."

"Because, parts of it are not for your scanning."

"I only require employment verification."

"We're being bossed around by a robot," said Drake. "Absurd."

"Ramon is just doing what he's been programmed to do, aren't you, Ramon?"

"That is correct, Miss Vivian."

Vivian reached into her purse, retrieved her card and handed it to Ramon. "Drake. You, too."

Reluctantly, Drake did the same. "So, what does this get us?"

"Mr. Drake, I do not understand your question. Please be more specific."

"What else can you tell us about Tess?"

"I have just confirmed your employment with your office and have determined that you are authorized to have this information. Tess left these premises at five twenty-seven P.M. yesterday, headed for Cond-Orbit for a meeting. She never made it as far as the IDT station. I have no further knowledge of her whereabouts."

Vivian was looking beyond Ramon, down the hallway. "Do you mind if we look around?"

"I am authorized to make that decision in her absence. You have the necessary clearance and are allowed to look, but not to touch. I will escort you in every room. But first, Mr. Drake, you must put that weapon back in its holster."

Ramon waited for Drake. When the gun was secured, he turned and headed for the hallway.

"Please, stay together."

"Thank you, Ramon. Drake? You coming?"

Drake followed Vivian down the hall, disliking the idea of being led around by the robot. Surely some sort of crime has been committed, he was thinking. Tess Altman has disappeared, without a trace so far, and the last person, in this case, robot, to see her was Ramon.

It is a suspect in a crime! And here it is, showing us what it wants us to see. You can't have a good investigation when a potential criminal, in this case, robot, is leading the investigation!

"Does anyone else live here?" Vivian asked, following Ramon into the study.

"No, Miss Vivian. The last two visitors into this house were you and Mr. Drake."

Ramon showed them the entire house, let them ask all of the questions that they wanted and carefully answered each one. It quickly became apparent to him that these two were on a fishing expedition, as Jordan would say. Yet, he also decided that they could be useful tools in his search for Tess.

By law, he was not allowed outside the house without a human. He could convince these two to take him to the park, even though he already knew the way, but predicted that one of two things would happen.

He would not be brought back, which would leave the house unprotected and him unavailable for further communications with Miss Tess, or the house would be more thoroughly searched in his absence, neither of which was acceptable. Better to guide them in his search for clues.

"Her normal route to the IDT station is through the park," Ramon volunteered. "Two blocks south of here. If she never made it, something happened to her in the park."

"I'd agree with that," said Vivian, turning, nudging Drake back the way they'd come. "Come on, Drake. Let's check it out. Ramon, thank you for your help. We may be back from time to time."

"You are authorized."

"If you have any news about Tess, can you contact me?"

"I will cooperate, Miss Vivian. May I ask the same of you? I am programmed to have concern for her safety."

Vivian smiled. "I will do that."

"Jesus," said Drake, heading for the door.

Ramon showed them out and locked up. Yes, he only required authorization for employment verification and toward that purpose he was satisfied.

But then his curiosity programming kicked in and within seconds, while talking to them and showing them the house, he also learned where they worked, how to contact them, what their job description was, who they worked for, and why.

Not that the card carried that much information. Rather, that it held the passwords and codes to those places that did.

These two were useful tools in his quest to find Tess and Jordan. He would now know as much as Miss Vivian, who always kept her recorder on and feeding back to a central computer. He could now monitor all of her conversations live.

And he had learned of the two accidents inside Cond-Orbit's dome. Operational Control reported two lightning strikes within the last forty-eight hours.

Lightning, Ramon learned early on, inside a dome is impossible. The superstructure is grounded. The solar cells inside that superstructure are all in a self-contained electrical system. Any charge attempting to get in from the outside would be grounded.

The only possibility of lightning would have to come from something already inside, charged, looking for a place to neutralize. A normal charge, with no intelligence, would just find ground and explode. A charge with intelligence and a will to survive would pick the spot, looking for the place least likely to cause an explosion.

The probe is inside the dome. Jordan is alive, needing assistance. Tess has disappeared, needing assistance. Cond-Orbit does not know where either of them are. Cond-Orbit works with a company that employs Miss Vivian and Mr. Drake. Their boss is a woman named Stella Powers.

And while gathering information about Stella's operation, Ramon discovered that he was being investigated by a spy-bot named Angel.

Locusts

Looking like a swarm of locusts moving in slow motion across the top of the dome, the mass went south, out over the fields of alfalfa and rows of corn, out over the thousands of other plants grown inside the dome and cast a fleeting shadow over the living things below.

Lingering over the dome's water recycling plant, the swarm began to drift downward, inching closer to the water, much to the dismay of the plant personnel.

The air should have been full of the buzzing sounds of millions of wings, not that any of those living inside the dome had ever seen a swarm of locusts up close, but the air was rumbling like it was going to explode.

They ran for cover, into the concrete pump stations, into the filtering buildings, over to the maintenance garage, to the main office, any shelter, and stared out of the windows.

As the mass drifted lower, the water became agitated and began to shake as if an earthquake were trembling below, splashing higher as the two bodies came together and adding a waterfall sounding roar to the mix.

Lightning flashed between water and cloud, accompanied with a burst of steam and a loud hissing sound. A clap of thunder rattled the windows, causing everyone to move away from the glass.

A dark mist filled the air, a hectic fog over an angry lake, a turbulent dark cloud hiding whatever was taking place inside.

They tried to call for help. But all communications links were down, all controls for filtering and pumping were temporarily disabled and power went down. All anyone could do was watch.

And then it was gone, just like that. Steam disappeared back into the dome's warm air as the water settled back down into a calm state, tiny ripples drifting toward the shoreline.

Questions, questions, questions

"Hi Malcolm. Pierce, here, Operational Control."
"Hi Pierce. What's up?"
"We had another incident. We need to talk."
"What kind of incident?"
"A black cloud hovered over the lake at the water recycling plant this morning, knocked out all of the power, communications, scared the hell out of everybody."
"Any idea what caused it?"
"Not yet. I was hoping you could help me out."
"I don't know what to say, Pierce. You think it's the same thing that took out the antenna tower?"
"Don't know why it wouldn't be. We didn't have this problem three days ago and now we've had it twice. My team has been over every inch of this dome and we haven't found a thing. The only place we haven't looked is in your facilities. That's why I'm making this call."
"I see. Well, all but one small section of Cond-Orbit's manufacturing facilities are available for your inspection at any time. Just give me a little advance notice and I'll have someone meet you at the entrance to show you around."
"Malcolm. You know we've already inspected those areas. It's that last section that I'm concerned about."
"I can't authorize that."
"And I can't let it go. I'm responsible for the safety of the people living and working inside this dome. If you've got something going on over there, I need to know about it."
"And my job is to ensure that this project remains low key and on track. Tell you what, Pierce. This is not something for us to decide. You take the issue

up on your side and if you can convince your upper management to talk to my upper management, so that they can instruct me to open this place up, I'd be happy to do that. How does that sound?"

"My upper management is in China."

"And mine is in orbit out in space. Something wrong with this picture?"

"OK, Malcolm. I'll run this up. But we need to keep this conversation ongoing."

"I'll go along with that. Can you send me the report on the last incident?"

"Done. Can you give me some kind of clue as to what the hell you're doing in there?"

"I wish I could."

"Malcolm, here."

"Malcolm? This is Tess."

"Tess?" Malcolm reached for a pen and something to write on. "Where are you?"

"With Lindy Moore."

"Lindy? Where?"

"I don't know."

"Jesus." Malcolm pushed the trace call option on his screen and waited for the results. Initial search showed no identifying numbers. He pushed the button again, twice this time, for a more thorough search. "What can I do?"

"Have there been any accidents in the dome since my last visit?"

"Accidents? Like..., what?"

"Anything out of the normal..., reportable. You know what I mean."

Malcolm leaned back in his chair with a sigh. "Yes. They've had a couple."

"They. Who are they?"

"Dome operations."

"What kind of accidents?"

Malcolm's screen reported back that the call could not be traced. "Lightning hit an antenna tower on the east side, burned up some equipment."

"Is that related to what I think it is?"

Malcolm sent an emergency message to Stella, requesting a trace. "Anything's possible at this point."

"What else?"

"Some kind of cloud hovered over the lake this morning, caused some commotion."

"Why do I sense that you're down playing this?"

"Jesus, Tess. I'm more worried about you. Does

Lindy have any demands? What's this all about?"

"Is it true that the probe is only capable of keeping Jordan alive for three more days?"

"Tess, this is an unsecured line."

"Tell me, Malcolm. I need to know. Even if Lindy is listening, which I suspect she is, she already knows all of this. I want to hear it from you."

Message from Stella: "Call is not traceable. Got Angel working on it."

Malcolm sighed. "Yes. That's true. Jordan has three more days. On the other hand, we don't know what time does over there. He might live a million years."

"And he might have vaporized the instant he left. We just don't know, do we? Those..., accidents. Is that Jordan trying to come back?"

"They don't know what it is."

"How about you?"

"You know what I think."

"Who has last say in allowing the probe to go full power?"

"I do. But I did not authorize it. Jordan did this on his own. Tess, we've got to get you back here, safe and sound. What do I have to do to make that happen?"

"I'm told that when the time comes, whenever that is, I'll be driven to a destination of my choice, alive, I hope."

"What does that mean? When the time comes."

"I don't know. Looks to me like you and Lindy need to talk. I'm just stuck in the middle. And I'm not liking it very much in case anyone's asking."

Message from Stella: "Malcolm, you won't believe this. The call is coming from several places at once. They're switching on and off from one connection to another. Most of them are coming in from the east, out near San Bernadino. But one of them came from inside the dome, your dome."

"Tess, is Lindy there?"

"No. She's out. I wanted her to be part of this call but when I heard that she was gone, I decided to call you. I'm sure she's going to contact you. Otherwise, what's the point?"

"Did she give any indication as to what she wanted?"

"Nothing specific."

"Anything I can do for you, Tess?"

"We're waiting on Lindy."

"Have you called the police?"

"Both you and Lindy share one common thought. Both of you want this to be kept quiet. Why is that?"

"That's what I'm being paid to do, Tess, keep it quiet, move it forward."

"And now I'm being held hostage. I don't feel like I'm in danger. More like a..., pawn."

"I understand that feeling, believe me. But I'm not the one holding you hostage. Go impress on that robot outside your door that time is wasting. Every second counts. Get it involved. Where is Lindy? Ask it that. Tell it you need to see Lindy now. And let's keep this line open, if you can. I'll be sitting right here."

Anthony glanced at his watch, took another sip of coffee and kept his eye on the door. Lindy was ten minutes late and he was beginning to wonder if she was going to show. It wouldn't be long before Malcolm noticed that he was not in the dome and then he would be asking questions.

Time is of the essence. Jordan's down to hours. He's out there. And he's aware of his situation. He's going to try again. It's just a matter of time.

Good luck, Malcolm. I think you've got yourself a full-blown situation.

Ball's in Lindy's court. Waiting on her.

He felt a hand on his shoulder and looked up to find Lindy, who gently rubbed her fingers over his cheek as she sat down in the chair next to him. Crossing her legs, he couldn't help but notice how short her skirt was. "I came in the side door."

"You look ravishing."

She smiled. "I try to keep up appearances, even though you have most of my clothes."

Anthony reached into his pocket and gave her a slip of paper with an address and a key to a locker. "And here is where you'll find them. They're all packed up and boxed."

"And it's under surveillance."

"Of course, not. We might be business partners. I wouldn't want to jeopardize that."

Lindy settled back in her chair and studied him. "Business partners..., to what extent?"

"I like your taste in clothes."

Lindy laughed. "Is that part of the deal?"

"Could be. Is that a deal breaker?"

"I don't know. Is it a deal maker?"

Anthony liked this cat and mouse game. The intrigue of it, sex with Jordan's lover while he lingered out in never-never land. He wasn't going to make it back anyway.

You were a fool, Jordan. Never go full power unless you know what's waiting for you. But you just had to be the first to know.

As the old saying goes, there are old test engineers and there are bold test engineers, but there are no old, bold test engineers. Too bad.

"Lindy, I'm going to stick with Cond-Orbit until it becomes untenable. How does that work for you?"

"Like I said, you can work for both of us. In fact, you might be the key player in all of this."

"How so?"

"I'm contacting Malcolm after our meeting. We both have a need for your services and those of Tess Altman. Have you met her, yet?"

"No, can't say as I have. What about Tess?"

"She is with us at the moment."

"I suspected that. It doesn't seem to bother you to sweep people off of the streets, does it?"

"I want the good guys to win."

"Right. We all have black hats and you've got the white ones. Problem is, I'm working for a company that is legally registered to do its work in this country. I'm not so sure about yours."

"It's a murky relationship, Tony. Maybe you should accompany me back to my facilities. I can explain it better over there."

Anthony smiled. "I might take you up on that..., later. First I've got to get back to the dome. Malcolm is becoming frantic. And he is the man I'm working for."

"When I speak with him should I mention our little conversation?"

"I would prefer that you didn't."

"It would hinder our business relationship?"

"Immensely. What are you going to do with Tess?"

"And my question would be, what are you going to do without her?"

"Touché."

Dome Operations

The Operations building was the highest inside the dome, four stories. The first floor was for the general public, getting permits, paying fees, handling the day-to-day basic operations of activities. Also, on the first floor, the cafeteria, company gym, and a few other concession stands that had open access to the courtyard.

The second floor was for the contractors, a place where they could bring their plans and hash out the details necessary to make one thing or another happen inside the dome. Small conference rooms were available, with reservations, and the floor was full of up-and-coming Cond-Orbit engineers who were working out of their cubicles.

The third floor was for senior engineers, their secretaries and other upper management. There was also a private gym, racket ball court, conference rooms and an upscale restaurant with a bar.

The forth floor was for Dome Operations. Pierce's crew worked here. This was where they kept track of everyone coming into and leaving the dome. It was the hub of operations, where the heads of the various departments kept their offices and where they could keep their fingers on the pulse of operations.

Looking out of the windows of his office, located on the south side of the building, Pierce could see all the way to the end of the dome, toward San Diego. Most of the year, except during the hot summer months, standing out on his balcony, he could watch the sun rise and set.

With binoculars, he discovered that he could see the recycling lake on the other side of the fields, but it would take a good telescope to get any good resolution. The first thing he'd done, after hearing about the cloud, was to go to the cameras mounted in the area and check their history.

They should have caught the action, but as the cloud approached the water, the signaling between the cameras and receivers went haywire and all that the monitors showed was fuzzy black and white static.

Pierce signaled for Joseph.

"Yes, sir?"

"Joseph. I need for you to purchase a telescope, something powerful enough to see to the other end of the dome, yet with a wide enough angle so that I can see a pretty good swath of land. Can you do that for me?"

"I'm on it. Any particular model?"

"Nothing cheap. I want quality. And I want it installed as soon as possible."

"Got it. Something with night vision capabilities?"

"Yes."

"Do you want to be able to see the images on your monitor?"

"Yes."

"Right. Do you want to be able to control it from your desk? You know, on a servomotor?"

"Yes."

"And do you want to be able to record what you see?"

"Of course! Joseph, you know what I'm looking for. Order it and get installed. Top Priority. Also, I want manual override capabilities so, if it comes right down to it, I have manual control."

"Got it. What do you expect to see?

"I don't know, Joseph. But if it's out there, I want to be able to see it with my own eyes. Are all alarms working properly..., throughout the dome?"

"Yes. We've tested all data points. Everything's OK."

"When was the last time the test was run?"

"This morning. And all cameras are working properly. We're ready to go."

"The cameras are going to be useless. The only way we're going to know is when we get alarms or if we get notified that they've stopped working. That'll give us the area."

"Hopefully, it's not over on the north side of the dome. You won't be able to see it with your telescope."

"Good point. Install two of them. One on the balcony outside of my office and the other one mounted on the railing on the north side, just outside the conference room. Link them both back to my computer."

Joseph knew he could have gotten away with installing just the one. But then, as luck would have it, the next problem would be on the north side and then he'd have to go through all of this again. Life was like that.

"Lindy Moore. So…, say what's on your mind."

"Hi Malcolm. I hear that you're having some problems over there."

"You heard wrong. Business as usual here."

"I'm not so sure. Sounds pretty serious to me. Took out an antenna site, huh?"

"Lindy. Let's get down to business. You have abducted a U. S. citizen, one of my employees, stolen our secrets and caused…,"

"Oh, get off your high horse, Malcolm. You have a disaster waiting to happen inside your dome and you're going to hang for it. What you should be doing is asking for my help. Let's start with that and then we'll negotiate from there."

"I'll just notify the police. You've already broken the law."

"And tell them what? That you've been running this secret project in the midst of the general public for the last ten years and, oh, by the way, it's gone awry and is probably going to blow up?"

"Everything's under control."

"Right. Everything except this little burst of energy that suddenly appears every now and then and blows things up. Wonder what that could be?"

"None of that is your concern. How do I get Tess back?"

"Providing that she wants to come back?"

"I'm sure that she does. No one wants to be held against their will."

"Actually, she's doing her investigating from here. The real problem, Malcolm, is Jordan. And the question is, how are you going to save him?"

"That stopped being your business a few days ago."

"It's very much my business. You are hoping for a miracle. I can help. But first, you have to lose that attitude."

"There is no way that you can help Jordan. You're a loser, a thief, a spy, and a kidnapper. Have you no shame for how low you can go?"

"Poor Malcolm. I can tell that you're under a lot of stress. I can help, but you're too busy focusing on the negative to see what I can provide."

"The best thing that you can do is release Tess..., now."

"And what would you do with her? You have no probe. You have no way to get hold of Jordan. He's going to sit out there until he runs out of time. And then he's going to make one last desperate attempt to come back and probably blow up the dome in the process. Tess isn't going to help."

"And I suppose that you have a plan?"

"I do. And it involves us working together. Do you think that you can do that?"

"Lindy, we were working together until I discovered your true loyalties. There is no reason for me to trust you now."

"See, Malcolm? There's your attitude getting in the way again. You'll have to work on that. Maybe you should take a self-improvement class, learn anger management and how to reason things out."

"All right. Say I go along with you. What's your plan?"

"That's more like it. I have two things that you desperately need. And you have one that I need just as badly. Together, we can be the heroes."

"The only thing that you have, that I want, is Tess. And you're holding her illegally."

"Here we go again. Malcolm, listen to what I'm saying. I - can - help. I'll pause while you let that sink in."

Malcolm sat back in his chair with a sigh.

Damn – this - bitch!

It's bad enough that she stole the plans, kidnaps Tess. Admonishes me for it. And holds me hostage for her actions!

"OK, Lindy. Spell it out. Time is wasting."

"What were you going to do with Tess? How was she going to be used?"

"I can't divulge that information."

"Right. Jordan's life hangs on a thread. And you're willing to sacrifice it in the name of company secrets."

"That's my job."

"Here's the deal, Malcolm. I have Tess. And I have a probe, exactly like Eclipse, just like the one that you lost."

"You have a *probe*?"

"And all of the apparatus that makes it shine. You, on the other hand, have nothing but problems that are going to make you famous. Now, are you ready to negotiate?"

"What is it that I have, that you want"

"I need Anthony Swincer's input."

"I cannot allow that."

"Right. I can understand that, company secrets and all. Tell you what. I'll let you think about it and call back in a couple of hours. I hope nothing goes boom between now and then. And I'll tell Tess that you're not ready to negotiate. Taa."

"Wait. What is it that you want from Anthony?"

"He is the one person that would know the final inputs to the probe. And he would know what your intentions are concerning Tess. I want his help."

"To do what? Launch another probe, if you even have one."

"Trust me, Malcolm. I have a probe. What I want to do is launch it."

"You don't have anyone that knows the controls, the procedures, the...,"

"It's all computer controlled. Jordan, we both know, had an override capability and took it full power. That saves your butt, right there. I will testify to that."

"But you don't know that, not for sure."

"What else could it be? We both heard it. The probe sounded differently on that last run. Remember how smooth that was, Malcolm? We can tell our computer to go full power once we know that final input. That's why I need Anthony."

"And who are you going to put in it?"

"I figured that you were going to use Tess."

"That's absurd! We would never put her in that kind of danger."

"Yet, you've included her in the project."

"You don't know that. You're on the outside, remember?"

"There you go again. Go take your medication. There's nothing else you could use Tess for. She doesn't know enough about the project."

"She doesn't need to," said Malcolm, thinking of her holographic memory system.

"Malcolm, let's cut the crap. I have a probe. You have Anthony. Our mutual interest is in seeing Jordan return safely. We both want the project to be a success. Our differences are in how the fortunes are going to be distributed and we don't have much time. Are you *listening*?"

Ramon set the coffee and sandwich on the table in front of Tess and then went around to the other side to watch her eat. "Miss Tess. I am pleased that you have come home. Would you care to discuss your journey?"

"You're going to hear all about it, Ramon. We're going to V-con with Lindy Moore, Anthony Swincer, and Malcolm."

"V-con, Miss Tess?"

"Virtual conference."

"May I inquire as to the purpose of this meeting, Miss Tess?"

"Lindy's company has a probe. But she needs Anthony's help to get it working. He works for Cond-Orbit."

"May I inquire as to why you are being included in this meeting, Miss Tess?"

Tess took a bite of her sandwich, chewed slowly, and swallowed before answering. "Jordan has modified my holographic memory system and added a telepathy converter and transducer. As usual, he has been sloppy and careless with where he stores the information. My job is to get the contraption to work."

"And have you been successful with that, Miss Tess?"

"I don't know. He took the other end of it with him. What an idiot."

"Miss Tess. May I offer a perspective?"

"Of course. I expect that from you, Ramon."

"I have listened to the recording of the conversation between Anthony, Malcolm, and Lindy when Jordan disappeared. And I have seen the video of the probe when it disappeared."

"Don't know how you got that information. I won't ask."

"All three agreed that the craft sounded better than at any time before, indicating a change implemented by someone, I suspect Jordan, shortly before lift-off. And just when the craft was programmed to shut down, Jordan put it under manual control and took it full power. This was a deliberate action."

"We all pretty much know this. Get to the point."

"Perhaps Jordan knew that you would be the only other person who would understand the complexities of the holographic memory system, especially under this time constraint."

"And?"

"Miss Tess , perhaps Jordan has a plan larger than what Malcolm and Lindy have in mind. Analyzing the circumstances that you are now in, I suspect that Jordan has included you in this project."

"Without even asking? That son of a..., Ramon, I don't need this!"

"It is purely a hypothesis, Miss Tess. I have no information indicating that Jordan knew of Lindy's probe, but that poses more questions. If he knew of it, he would also know, or at least have a good idea who was going to pilot it. If he did not know of Lindy's project, then he expected that his memory system...,"

"My memory system."

"I apologize, Miss Tess. He expected your memory system to work. Even if it did not, then he would also expect that you would be included in the project. This move of Jordan's forces everyone's hand."

"But why would he risk his life on an untested system?"

"I suspect that he thought it would work. There

may be more forces at work with this project than we are aware of. Miss Tess, you have not questioned this yet, but I am a prototype built by Jordan using your holographic memory system. I understand how it works and I already have the telepathy converter and transducer working. I might be of great assistance in helping to locate Jordan. Who is going to pilot this probe?"

"That hasn't been discussed. I'm not sure it needs one. It's supposed to be computer controlled. This whole thing's a crapshoot. What lunacy!"

"Miss Tess, will your memory system be installed in this probe with the telepathy transducer?"

"That would be my guess. I think that's what the meeting's all about."

"I apologize for being so inquisitive, Miss Tess. But does anyone have any idea which reality Jordan is in?"

"Everybody's clueless, Ramon. In any of an infinite number. I think I'll go take a waitress job up in Canada. That sounds simple, find a little cabin alongside a stream, go fishing in my spare time. I don't want this."

"And you also believe that you are not being compensated enough for your efforts."

"True. I don't know why I should take on this stress, especially at my pay level."

"That would be correct, Miss Tess. I've done a pay comparison and...,"

"I don't want to hear it. I can't say Jordan's worth it. Yet, I can't just stand by and let him die either."

"If I may have some input, Miss Tess. I have noticed that when you and Jordan were together, both of you were happier than when you were apart."

"How do I know that he didn't program you to say that? He's the one that gave you all this flipping knowledge. Who am I to trust?"

"He gave me all of these capabilities to protect you, Miss Tess. May I make a suggestion? Request that I be allowed to pilot Lindy's probe if their testing proves to be successful. Make that a condition of your involvement."

"Not a bad idea."

"There are calls coming in, Miss Tess. Your meeting is about to begin."

The call was held within WebMeet's virtual space. Different "offices" were available, mountain peaks, sunny beaches, stormy seas, war zones, sitting on the moon. Malcolm chose a small, plain room, square table in the center and with a chair on each side. Tess sat across the table from Lindy, Malcolm on her right, seated so that he faced Anthony.

"We have a lot to discuss," said Malcolm. "So I suggest that we get right to it. Lindy has proposed that Anthony be allowed to work with her team to make the second probe operational. Both companies will share this information. Anthony, you think you can make the probe functional?"

"I believe so. I'm just waiting for the OK to move ahead."

Malcolm turned to Tess. "What's the latest on Jordan's telepathy converter?"

"Jordan has the other end of it. I'm transmitting but getting no response."

"We can install it in Lindy's probe," said Anthony. "That might increase our chances."

"My question," said Tess, leaning forward to rest her chin on her hands, elbows on the table. "If Jordan is actually in a parallel universe and can't receive either yours or my signals, what makes you think that the probe will go to the same universe that Jordan is in? Isn't that what has to happen in order for this to work?"

"There are no guarantees," said Anthony. "That's what we're trying to find out. Jordan's leaving is way premature. All we're trying to do now is get him back."

"Do any of you believe that Jordan is still alive?"

Lindy, Malcolm, and Anthony exchanged glances.

"Of course, I do," said Malcolm.

"If anyone can pull something like this off," said Lindy, with a smile. "It'll be Jordan. I think he's still out there."

"I agree," said Anthony. "But he doesn't have much time."

"I have a suggestion," said Tess. "Since the holographic memory system is my baby, providing that the probe works and passes all tests, I would like my robot, Ramon, to pilot it."

"Put a robot in the probe?" said Malcolm. "For what purpose?"

"He just informed me that he already has a holographic memory system, a modification made by Jordan."

Anthony glanced over at Malcolm. "How about a telepathy transducer? Does he have that?"

"I don't know," Tess lied, hoping to steer away from that part of the conversation. "And if the probe tests successfully, and if Ramon advises me that it can sustain life, I'm going with it."

"No way," said Malcolm. "I can't authorize that."

"But I can," said Lindy. "Why don't you come work for me? I'll double your salary and give you a signing bonus."

Malcolm leaned back in his chair and buried his hands into his hair. "We're getting off target. Tess, it's not safe for you to go. There hasn't been enough testing. We don't know what happens over there."

"If the probe tests successfully under computer control," Tess continued, "I want Ramon to precede me with a test flight. If he reports back that the probe is functional, I go and he goes with me."

"There's barely enough space inside for you," said Lindy. "How big is this robot?"

"Slightly smaller than Judd."

"No way. Not enough room."

"You could cut back on the air supply," said Anthony, leaning back in his chair. "If Jordan's only got a couple of days left, why does Tess need a seven day supply? Cut it down to three. Extra space goes to Ramon."

"That would put the robot in the pilot position," said Lindy. "We don't have enough time to change the control panel."

"It won't matter," said Anthony. "It's all computer controlled as long as no one puts it into Manual."

"Does this probe have that capability?"

"Yes," Lindy, nodded.

"And, before we launch, I want Ramon to have access to all documents relating to the probe."

There was a quick exchange of glances around the table and some general mumbling and shaking of heads this way or that.

"I can't authorize that," said Malcolm, at last.

"But I can," said Lindy. "Sure..., let's do it."

"They're not your plans to give away," said Malcolm, his voice rising.

"You two have no choice," said Anthony. "Tess did not ask for permission. She stipulated one of the conditions that had to be met before she agrees. Right?"

"Yes."

"May I make a suggestion?" said Anthony, sitting up. "I think Tess deserves compensation from both companies, since she'll working for both. Malcolm?

117

Would you give her some sort of extra compensation? She is, after all, going to be risking her life."

"I can make that happen. But she's not going."

"Lindy, would you match the salary that she gets from Cond-Orbit?"

"I can do that."

"Then, it's a deal," said Tess.

Tess knew her blood pressure was high. She could feel it, heart pumping much faster than normal, kind of a rush behind her eyes and a high pitched ringing in her ears. Yep. She was stressing.

"It's all computer controlled," they said. "All you have to do is sit there and transmit."

It was a four-hour class, learning where specific controls were located, should there be an emergency, how to reset coordinates, emergency instructions for reestablishing contact with the base, backup power systems, and on and on. Tess strapped herself in.

"OK, Ramon. You've already taken this thing for a joy ride. What can I expect?"

"Miss Tess, all life support systems and their back-ups are in working order and you have seventy-two hours of air. The process that takes place takes place at the speed of light so there will be no chance for you to have any reaction."

"And then, what?"

"Since we will be traveling at the speed of light, that moment of time is infinite for us. During that interval, we will have a chance to choose which reality we wish to visit. We have to find the one that has Jordan in it."

"How are you going to do that?"

"I noticed that this probe's computer programming is primitive in one fundamental principle. It does not have curiosity. That means that its task is to propel the probe out into the unknown without regard as to precisely where it will land. Since that is a crap-shoot, as you have said, I will take control of our probe at that moment."

"Put it in Manual?"

"Yes, Miss Tess."

"That goes against everything I just learned. Ramon. Are you sure?"

"I have already accomplished that task, Miss Tess, during the last run. It is much like hitting the "Pause" button in whatever program is running. This is an acceptable situation. We will be in limbo until we make a decision as to where we will go. Time does not exist at that moment so we will have forever to find Jordan."

"But I only have three days of survival."

"That is correct, Miss Tess. I will be monitoring all of your life support systems continuously."

"What am I doing here, Ramon? Am I crazy?"

"Do not concern yourself with such thoughts, Miss Tess. Where you are going will make this life seem infinitesimally small and insignificant in comparison."

"It seems pretty important, right now."

"That would be correct, Miss Tess, because you are trapped within this time line. That will change shortly. If you are ready, Miss Tess, push the button. They will finalize all tests, ensure that all systems are a go and then power up."

"I wish I had your ability to absorb all of this information. You did that so quickly."

"I do not have emotions or distractions to distort my input, Miss Tess. Humans have a need to categorize in an illogical way. My process is more efficient. All I've done is record. Analysis and categorizing will occur in real time as the need arises."

"OK, Ramon. Let's do it. If I don't make it, you've been a great friend."

"I am here for you, Miss Tess."

Tess paused as she held her hand over the button. If she didn't push it, she figured that she had another sixty years of pretty good living, maybe more if she continued on with her health regime. Living to be a hundred was pretty much commonplace and with medicine able grow and replace defective parts, healthy living up to a hundred was likely.

Countering that, filtering of both air and water on a house-by-house basis was becoming necessary with single and multi-family domes becoming the new standard of acceptable living, so much more efficient than a house, especially the old, wooden frame houses that had been built up until the last fifty years.

Malcolm is right. Earth is slowly being evacuated. People are moving on. Life in space is cleaner, easier, more disease and crime free and the upwardly mobile population is leaving in droves. Better to get away from Earth before it goes.

So, here I am, thirty-two, without anything great in my life to speak of. Family's gone, not too many friends, and the one person I care about the most, who left me, is in limbo out in never-never land, needing my assistance. Is that worth pushing this button?

"I detect that you are having doubts, Miss Tess. If you have changed you mind I will initiate that action."

"It's a lot of money, they're offering."

"Thanks to your hard bargaining, Miss Tess. You will be able to purchase a dome."

"I've never been out in space. Maybe I'll buy a place up in orbit."

"I predict that, should you be successful, your entire life will change. Opportunities will abound."

"Where we're going, is there going to be gravity?"

"You will be a part of gravity, Miss Tess, just like you will be part of all the forces that make up that particular moment, all things in some way connect-

ed. You will feel nothing and everything simultaneously, until we pick the next reality."

"Have you been to one, yet?"

"No, Miss Tess. I have confirmed that the probe is
functional. Where we go is up to you."

"So..., instead of downloading a video, we'll be up-
loading ourselves into some other place?"

"That is my prediction."

Tess looked at the gauges and displays laid out
before her and then switched to the screen showing
Malcolm, Anthony, and Lindy in the control booth,
watching anxiously.

Then she switched to the camera that was aimed at
the probe, to the area of the probe where she was sitting, saw an image of herself looking up and pushed
the button.

Pierce put the call up on his screen. Zodi, sitting in the cab of her truck, was looking into the dash-cam and pointing up. "Pierce? Zodi, here. Can I call you Pierce?"

"You can call me anything. Just tell me what's going on."

"There's an odd mist above the antenna site right now. Never seen anything like it."

Pierce clicked the telescope icon on his monitor and a split view, one looking north and one south, popped up. "What site are you at?"

"Twelve, the southernmost site inside the dome."

"OK. I'm bringing the area in. Describe this mist."

"Right now, it's reflecting the color of the sun. I've seen it darker, just a couple of minutes ago. It is definitely inside the dome."

"OK. I think I'm getting it. You're beyond the recycling lake, right?"

"Yes. The mist appears to be about a hundred feet across, but that changes by the minute."

"How high? Oh. There it is! I see it. Looks like it's a couple hundred feet above you. Have you seen any sparks or heard anything that sounds like electricity?"

"Not yet. But if this is anything like Site Six, it'll have to get closer to the antenna first. That's when sparks start to fly."

Pierce signaled for Joseph to join him in the control room. Then he left a message for Malcolm to call in as soon as possible.

Good. Getting this recorded. I'll have some video for Malcolm to explain. He can't deny this.

"Zodi. Do you feel like you are in any kind of danger? Cause if you do, I want you to get out of there."

"Adan says it goes for ground, like that antenna tower. I'm pretty sure I'll be safe in my truck. It's got rubber tires."

"You are in your truck now, right?"

"Yes. I'm turning to get a better look at it."

"Stay in contact with me, Zodi. I've got a couple of people I want to join us. Malcolm, you here?"

"I'm here."

"Joe? You on here?"

"No, sir," said Joe. "I'm standing right behind you. I was across the hall."

"Malcolm? I'm going to share these images with you. OK, coming at you."

"Got it. What is that?"

"I was hoping you could tell me."

"Never seen anything like it."

Pierce leaned back in his chair and used the remote to increase power on the scope. "Zodi, looks like it's coming down toward ground. Why don't you get out of there?"

"It's coming down? It doesn't look like it from here."

"Trust me. It is. Get out of there."

"Right. Getting warm inside the truck, anyway. OK. Pedal's to the metal."

Pierce leaned forward, staring at the screen. "The cloud's compressing, heading down. Are you seeing this, Malcolm?"

"I'm seeing it. I just don't know what to say."

"It's got nothing to do with your project?"

"Not that I can tell."

"Zodi? Is that as fast as your truck goes?"

"Well, they're underpowered and we gotta carry all of this equipment. They're slugs. Getting hot in here. What's that thing doing, Pierce?"

"It's down to about a hundred feet above you."

"Sky's getting kind of dark. Is it following me? What the hell? I've got rubber tires!"

"Not necessarily true," said Joseph, glancing over at Pierce. "Carpool started replacing some of the old, worn out rubber tires on the vehicles with some kind of new synthetic ones. I read it in Cond-Orbit News about a month ago."

"I just had new tires put on this truck! What the hell?"

"Zodi. You're heading toward a heavily populated area. If that cloud's following you, I recommend that you head east or west and stay in the agricultural area."

"Oh..., so I can experience this all by myself? OK. I'm heading west. And I want a pay raise. What's it doing, Pierce?"

"Looks like you're OK. It's closing in on the antenna tower."

"These synthetic tires. Do they have any metal in them?"

"Whoa!" Joseph pointed at the monitor. "Did you see that? Lightning hit the tower!"

Pierce, speaking slowly and calmly, said, "Malcolm. I'm going to notify the police and let them come into the dome and investigate unless you talk to me, right now."

"You can't let them come in. The dome operates under its own rules. You open up the dome to the police, your company will be violating the terms of the contract. That will not go down well for you, or your company."

"Jesus, Malcolm! Tell me what the hell is going on. There is no other explanation for this. I have to know. Should I evacuate the dome?"

"Cloud's going back up," said Joseph. "I've notified Security. We've got three vehicles closing in on the

125

area now."

"Why?" said Pierce. "What are you going to do? Shoot it? Zodi? Looks like it's coming your way."

"Maybe I'll just put this thing in a low gear, point it south and jump out. What do you think, guys?"

"Definitely don't do that," said Pierce. "We don't need your truck plowing into the dome. If you want to park it, get out and go for shelter, you have my permission."

"I'm driving alongside a cornfield."

"Malcolm?" said Pierce. "How quickly can you get over here?"

"I'm afraid that I can't at the moment."

"What's more important than this? For Christ's sake, Malcolm."

"I'm not in the dome."

"Where are you? I'll send a vehicle."

"I am not available at the moment. I will notify you as soon as I am. And I will get there as soon as I can. That's the best I can do, Pierce."

"Crimanently! Joseph, notify your people to turn away all non-essential personal attempting to enter the dome. All those who are leaving, stay gone until further notice. Other than essential maintenance and security personal, I want the dome empty in the next twenty-four hours. You hear that, Malcolm?"

"You gotta do what you gotta do, Pierce. I'll get back to you when I can. Good luck, everybody."

"Zodi, here. Sky's getting dark. I'm going to take my chances inside the truck."

For the hundredth time in the last hour, Jordan glanced down at the instrument panel. Air supply, normal, oxygen normal, power availability, normal, all pumps, ventilation ducts, filters, life support systems, normal.

Everything OK. What the hell? Why is there no homing signal? Why doesn't the probe know where it's supposed to go?

According to all of our estimations, the probe never should have left the stand! All I know is the probe is not where it's supposed to be.

There's supposed to be a trailer. They're supposed to be able to track me. Why isn't that working?

Thirty-seven hours and fifty-five minutes to go.

"Malcolm? Eclipse to Cond-Orbit. Anybody read me?"

Of course, not. Not if they don't know where, or when, I am. It's impossible for our signals to connect. If we could talk they could locate my position.

"Eclipse to Cond-Orbit. Hello. Anybody out there? Malcolm?"

OK. I'm on my own. I've gone back to the navigational start point. But it's not there, not the place I left, apparently.

Every time I start to enter, huge power-drain. We're supposed to equalize. Not blow each other up.

Can't see what's happening until I enter. I have to commit before I can see.

I'm pretty sure I'm still in the dome. Just don't know

where. If I bring it in, it's gonna go boom. Bad luck? Or espionage? You choose.

Stuck on the doorstep. The problem has to be in the programming. Yet, we went over everything again and again.

Lindy. Lindy Moore. Knew she was a spy. Didn't think she knew enough to screw things up.

"Eclipse to Cond-Orbit. I'm going to make another attempt to bring this baby in. Malcolm? Are you reading me? Anybody read me?"

Zodi

There was nothing Zodi could do. The truck stopped of its own accord. Turn the key whatever way you want. Try and turn the lights on or off, or make a phone call, or even honk the horn. Nothing. It wasn't going to happen.

And then the sky turned dark and it began to rain, not water and not down. Soil began to rise up to meet the cloud, little columns of dirt, boiling up from the earth, rising up toward this new thing that was between them and the top of the dome.

Zodi peered out through the windshield and out the side windows and out the back, staring at the things in the bed of her truck. The tools that were not strapped down began bouncing higher than they should even though the truck was coming to a halt.

And then the tools were up in the air along with the cornstalks and the fence and the truck and the road, all of them rising, a sickening feeling in the gut, rising up to meet the cloud. The headlights flashed on and off while the truck alarm wailed into the dust that was everywhere. Static bristled in the thick air.

And then the dust was in the cab. Zodi watched in horror as the images of the things close to her, the dashboard, the steering wheel, her hands in front of her face, began to disappear into the dust.

Ten thousand angels began to sing into the explosive air, a steady note that sounded like forever.

"Ramon, I'm freaking out. I can't see anything."

"That would be correct, Miss Tess. The ability of humans to react to a new set of realities is far less than desirable."

"I mean I can't *see* anything. I can't *feel* anything. I can't *smell* anything. I'm going crazy. Any minute now, I'm going to scream!"

"That would be illogical, Miss Tess. Screaming would serve no purpose."

"Yes..., it would."

"I propose that you save your energy, Miss Tess. Three days in this probe will completely exhaust you. I predict that you will be able to see in a few moments. There is light outside the probe but it is not in a frequency that your eyes can detect. I am working to adjust the probe's sensors so that a conversion will take place that allows that to happen. Please be patient."

"What do you see, Ramon?"

"I see possibilities."

"What does that mean?"

"It means that you will experience nothing, other than what takes place inside this probe, until our next moment is determined."

"Nothing? But I'm thinking thoughts. Things are happening. Right?"

"Only inside the probe, Miss Tess. As an example, do you feel gravity at this moment? That was one of your questions earlier."

"Um, now that you mention it, no."

"Nor will you hear anything outside this probe. Nor will you be able to touch anything."

"Why not?"

"Because we are a part of everything that makes up this moment. We are in a pure energy state. As soon as we pick a new reality, this moment will be gone. And then you have a new set of things to experience."

"Just don't stop talking, Ramon. I could go nuts here, very easily. I'm on the edge already."

"We've only been gone five minutes. You have another four thousand, three hundred and fifteen minutes left to find Jordan."

"You know what? I don't think I care. Let's go back. How hard is it to do that?"

"Miss Tess, I must question your honesty when you answered the loyalties question. You stated that you were happiest when with Jordan, but your resolve to help him lasts only five minutes?"

"So..., what? I had no idea what I was getting into. I think I'd rather have a quiet sixty years back home, even if I don't live in a dome, even if I don't live with Jordan. There are lots of guys out there that find me very attractive. If Jordan hadn't *left* me, Ramon, things would be different. Do you understand what that means?"

"We have already had this conversation, Miss Tess. Jordan left to resolve the problems occurring with his work, not because of anything to do with you."

"How do I know that you're not programmed to say that?"

"I have been programmed to keep you safe and happy, Miss Tess. And to that end, I have adjusted this probe's sensors to this new set of circumstances. If you will note, light is becoming visible to you."

"I would like to see something. My imagination is going crazy and taking me with it. Human beings cannot be sensory deprived and I certainly am one that..., oh, very faint. I can hardly tell that I see it. I feel like my eyes are playing tricks on me. Is it really light? Or, is this my imagination?"

"It is real, as viewed through the sensors of this probe."

"Light is coming from…, everywhere. It's beautiful!"

"We are a part of the light, Miss Tess. There is no source and hence, no shadow. We are all components of the glow, the energy of this moment outside of time. Would you like to take a minute or two to appreciate that?"

"Can you make it brighter?"

"I am adjusting slowly, so as not to startle you. Soon, Miss Tess, you will be able to see objects inside the probe. But they will not look the same as you remember them. They will be sources of energy, not matter, as you know it."

"I can see my hands. I can see through them!"

"That would be correct, Miss Tess. We are pure energy…, with a purpose. If, and when, you are ready, we will begin our search for Jordan."

Hallelujah

After the cloud lifted, Zodi found herself sitting in the driver's seat of her truck, just as if nothing had happened. Looking out the back window, all of her tools were in place, nothing missing as best as she could tell without getting out and checking, which she had no intention of doing.

The truck started up fine, the electric motor purring quietly as she made a U-turn in the road and headed north, back toward the populated parts of the dome. While she was reestablishing contact with Pierce she tried to remember, exactly, what had happened.

Certainly being lifted up into the cloud was real. She could not imagine that it did not happen because she saw it with her own eyes. On the other hand, she couldn't believe that it did.

After that..., what? I remember something about a light, a brightly glowing light coming out of the sky, engulfing me, holding me.

See? That makes no sense! But that is what I felt. Did I die? Was I dying?

Apparently not, because here I am. I remember angels singing..., angels. And..., that light.

I was in the presence of The Lord!

Yes!. I remember now. He told me to trust in Him. Even though I was seized by the Cloud of Death, I should fear no evil, for Thou art with me.

I've been saved! Trust in Him and believe in Him and you shall be saved!

Hallelujah!

"Pierce, here. Zodi? Are you OK?"

"I am fine. And it's a wonderful day! Praise the Lord!"

"What? What happened inside the cloud?"

"I'm heading north, Pierce, toward your office. Looking out my windshield, it looks like the cloud is coming your way."

"Yes. We're watching it on the monitor. What happened inside the cloud?"

"I talked to God. Well, not quite. But I felt His Presence and I was saved."

"Right..., Zodi, I want you to report into the hospital. I'll have a couple of doctors meet you there. We want to give you a complete going over and make sure you're OK."

"I'm fine, never felt better."

"I'm glad you're safe. I still want you to go to the hospital. Our connection is starting to break up. The cloud is getting close."

"Embrace it, Pierce! Embrace the Holy Cloud and you will be saved!"

What It Isn't

The cloud was close enough now that they could see it without the aid of the telescope. It was still high in the dome and scattered so that it cast only a slight shadow over the area below.

From the perspectives of the people outside the buildings, walking around, buying snacks, having coffee in the park by the fountain, getting along with the day's business, everything looked the same. Clouds passed over the dome all the time, casting thin shadows.

Watching from the balcony, Joseph turned back into the room. "I think we should sound an alarm."

Pierced laughed, sarcastically. "Right! You'll have a thousand people getting trampled at the gates. No, Joseph. We have to keep this quiet. We have to have everyone leave in some kind of orderly fashion."

"But..., if this thing comes down to ground level, people are going to get killed."

"How many people have been killed so far?"

"Well..., none. But even one is too many."

"Joseph, why do we pay you so much? If we sound an alarm, people are going to stand around and ask each other, "What's that for?" They're not going to know what to do. If..., and when, they see the cloud coming down, they'll run for cover. It's instinctual."

"Don't they deserve some kind of warning?"

"What alarm do we have that says that there is something inside the dome with us, we don't know what it is, or what it's going to do, but we suggest that you take cover, even though we don't think that's going to help either, but don't panic, everything's under control and please don't rush the gates because someone might get crushed. Oh. And by the way, keep it hush-hush, according to Malcolm."

"Sir, your monitor just went out."

"I expected that. OK. Let's get over to the scope. I want to see it with my own eyes, up close."

"Looks like that might happen," said Joseph, stepping back out onto the balcony. It's coming in."

"Ahh. There it is. Now, if I can just keep it in focus."

Pierce spent another few minutes attempting to do just that. "Hmm. Take a look at this, Joseph. Tell me what you see."

Squinting into the scope, Joseph watched the motion, or lack of it, as the cloud moved closer. "I don't know how to describe it. It looks like there are things making the shadows and distorting the light. But when I try to see what that thing looks like, it just becomes air again..., like that thing was never there."

"That's what I thought. It's not moving. More like disappearing and then reappearing."

"Right. What is it?"

"Malcolm's cloud. Damn it! He should be here. Find out where that call came from. I want to know where he is."

"Right. What about the cloud? Are you going to stay up here?

"No, Joseph. I thought I'd go down to the basement headquarters. I want you to stay here and defend the building."

"What?"

Pierce smiled. "Come on. Let's get out of here."

Stepping from the balcony, heading back through the office, they discovered that the lights had gone out, that the entire room had lost power and that the security doors leading out to the hallway had closed in the locked position. Pierce ran back to his desk, grabbed a chair and, rolling it in front of him, crashed it through the glass door.

Lightning crackled between the cloud and the building as the two touched, a brilliant flash of light accompanied by an explosion. Thunder echoed through the structures below, across the patio, over the land and, seconds later, returned as a low, distant rumble. Everybody ran for cover.

Appearing inside the room without ever entering through an open door or window, the cloud became part of the walls, the security doors, various sections of the stairwell heading down.

Holding the flashlight steady on the steps, going down, taking two at a time, Pierce saw the cloud appear in front of him, tiny fragments of the stairs and walls disappearing and then reappearing as other parts fell away.

He turned and headed back up the stairs, until he saw Joseph, who was coming down, disappear into the cloud. Seconds later, he too, was swept up, freed of this world and becoming part of something new.

"I am still interpreting this data, Miss Tess. So, please be patient."

"What happened, Ramon? Everything just went black."

"I predict that we have reached the outer limits of this time slot."

"I'm freaking out. Do something."

"We don't want to do something irrational, Miss Tess. I predict that even infinity is not so exact. Humans speculate that this moment in time is precise, but apparently that is not true. Slippage appears to be part of the process."

"Speak in my terms, Ramon."

"We are in limbo between two realities, the one you left and the one you'll choose. The time slot that keeps us in-between is slipping away and, since we have not chosen a new reality, we're going to become part of something else."

The sun rose up out of the east, looking more like it was painted than real, glowing softly behind the smoke-filled air, fuzzy around the edges.

"Ramon. Where are we?"

"We are still on Earth. Refreshed data shows that we have never moved from the original launch point. I am currently recalculating our place in time. I have not yet decoded their information delivery system."

"We're in the same place? How?"

"In a different time."

"And, what year is it?"

"I am still calculating. My analysis of the air outside our capsule is breathable. But I do not recommend that we exit."

"Good. Cause I'm not getting out. What if something attacks us while we're here?"

"I predict that we have moved into the future, initial readings are proving that...,"

"What the hell am I doing here, Ramon? Why did I let you talk me into this? This was all part of one big plan, wasn't it? Jordan had this all worked out from the beginning. Didn't he? Tell me the truth."

"Jordan cares for you very much. He...,"

"Oh, bull shit!"

"It appears that our place in time is approximately one hundred years in the future."

"And what is the purpose of this trip? The stupidity of sending a human into the flipping unknown! And I volunteered, thanks to you, Ramon."

"Ninety-seven years, four months, and seven days. The unanswered question, Miss Tess, is why are we outside now? This probe was launched from an underground site."

"No. The unanswered question is, what are we still doing here? I want to go back."

"I do not detect any danger to your well-being, Miss Tess. And my curiosity programming is engaged in our present situation. When we entered Lindy Moore's launch site, I took GPS coordinates and altimeter readings. After entering her facilities, we dropped ninety feet down to get to the probe. Yet, here we are at the same altitude and in the same place, but we see sky."

"And you're wondering *why*?"

"That is correct. I...,"

"You're just like Jordan! I should've known he'd program an obstinate robot. Ramon, I want you to leave right now. It's obvious that Jordan is not here."

"Someone is. Our probe is being approached."

"I thought you could detect stuff like that."

"I am detecting it, Miss Tess. These are not humans. Rather, some type of android. Their technology is excellent. They have masking."

"What does that mean?"

"I cannot detect their intentions. I can barely detect their presence."

"Why aren't we leaving? Go, Ramon."

"I am powering back up. We will be at full power in one hundred and twenty seconds."

"When did you power down? You need to let me know those things! No more surprises."

"They have weapons, Miss Tess. But they are not drawn. Act calm."

"Act calm?"

"Greetings, Human. We mean you no harm. We approach as friends."

Tess sank into her seat. "Jesus. Ramon? Do we have any weapons onboard?"

"I would not think such thoughts, Miss Tess. These androids have telepathic capability. I am currently masking our mission and your thoughts with an encrypted shield. But you must remember, technology has improved greatly in the last one hundred years. I cannot predict how long I will be able to keep them out."

The androids approached the windows on either side of the probe and peered inside. The one on Tess' right, spoke first. "Hello. I am Jackson, ranger in charge of this area. Assisting me, is Jeanette. Please identify yourself."

Tess took a deep breath, composed herself, and looked over at Jackson. "I am Tess Altman, citizen of the United States."

"Tess Altman, do you realize that you have placed your vehicle on the very spot of the Catastrophe of

Twenty-One-Thirty-two?"

"I'm sorry, I didn't know."

"Miss Tess. This is Ramon. Please inquire about the catastrophe. It might aid us in our search for Jordan."

"Um, what happened in twenty-one-thirty-two?"

"You are unaware of the explosion? It took out half of the mountain."

"I.., I'd heard about it, but didn't pay much attention. What happened?"

"There was a secret facility inside the mountain. They were experimenting with parallel universe technology but miscalculated the energy fields."

"Just like the one that took out the Cond-Orbit dome down in the valley," said Jeanette, talking from the other side."

Jackson tapped on the glass. "I am not getting validation of your identity. Would you please show me some identification?"

"How did you get here?" Jeanette asked. "There are no roads and I don't see that this craft has any type of propulsion."

"Um..., yes. That would be correct."

"Miss Tess, tell them that we are a top-secret test probe for the U. S. Government. Take control."

"I cannot show identification because I am involved in a top-secret project for the U. S. Government."

"Your vehicle has no identification. We must record all visitors to this area. Therefore...,"

"You don't understand top-secret? If it's top secret, why would I carry identification? I must insist that you keep all knowledge of this encounter quiet. Do you understand?"

"I am requesting protocol, Tess Altman. Please wait."

"Tess Altman?" said Jeanette, drawing her weapon. "That was the name of the test pilot involved in that catastrophe. Are you *that* Tess Altman?"

"*We are at full power, Miss Tess. I predict that this encounter will delay our search for Jordan and that it will end badly. Shall we resume our journey?*"

"Get me the hell out of here, Ramon!"

Clarence

Malcolm and Anthony were stopped at the underground entrance back into Cond-Orbit. The guard
had seen them approaching and turned off the auto-
entry feature, giving him full control. Stopped at the
gate, Malcolm directed his attention to the blind tint,
bulletproof glass.

"Hello. Anybody in there?"

"Clarence, here. How may I help you?"

"The gate's not opening."

"That's because it's turned off."

"I'm authorized. I have full clearance for the entire
dome."

"I see that. It's showing up on my screen. But I
have orders not to allow anybody inside."

"Well, Clarence, that might apply to everyone else,
but not me and not to my associate here, Anthony
Swincer. Open the gate."

"I am sorry, sir. I have my orders."

"Who ordered that?"

"The head of Security."

"That would be Joseph?"

"Yes. Except he's not getting back to me. I've been
trying to contact him. Me, and every other guard
around the dome, so's we can get the rest of the
message."

"What message?"

"Says here, "Do not allow anyone back inside the
dome except...,"

"Except..., what?"

"I don't know. None of us got the rest of the message."

"Well, he meant me! I'm the exception!"

"Well, I'd like to agree with you. And you're certain-

143

ly acting like it should be you. But I got my orders."

"You don't have any orders!"

"Like I said, I'm obeying the part I've got. I'm waitin' on the rest."

"Clarence, you have to understand what I'm going to say. It is urgent, and I mean exactly that, urgent, imperative, whatever conveys to you the utmost importance that I get inside the dome. And it has to happen, *now*!"

"Problem is, the rest of the order could say, "except Malcolm and associates. Shoot them on sight. I won't know until I get the rest of my orders. You see the exit over there? Everybody, and I mean everybody else is leaving. And you want to go in? I gotta ask myself, why?"

"It doesn't matter *why* to you! You don't need to know why, only that you do the one thing that you're paid to do, make sure that I get in and out of the dome as I please! Got it? Now open the gate!"

"I am sorry, sir. But I have my orders. Now, if he had said everybody except Malcolm, I could accept that. But he didn't. He's the man I work for."

"And he works for me! Damn it! I'll have your job...,"

"Wait," said Anthony, pointing to the windowless steel door to their right, about twenty feet away. "This is getting nowhere. Clarence, do you have access to that door over there?"

"I do."

"Can you meet me there?"

"I can do that."

Malcolm alternated between thumping his fingers nervously on the wall and wringing his hands as he watched Anthony and Clarence talk at the door. He couldn't hear anything due to the commotion of everyone else leaving.

This was not like the normal exit of people. These

workers were carrying tools, personal items, things that they thought might be hard to replace if something went wrong. Apparently, that is exactly what they thought.

Anthony tapped him on the shoulder, motioned to the open gate and then looked up at the camera. "Thanks, Clarence. Good man. I'll make sure it happens."

Malcolm hurried through, hoping the guard wouldn't change his mind at the last second, and then proceeded over to Transportation. "What did you tell him?"

Anthony laughed. "That the thing that was causing everyone else to leave could only be controlled by you and that you were going to be the hero...,'

"Or the sacrificial goat."

"And that he could play a large part of the event by bucking the chain of command and letting you in."

"He bought that? What else?"

"That he could turn off the cameras for a second or two and let us slip in unobserved. That way, if things did go wrong, it couldn't be traced back to him."

"But that's not true. The scanner knows who comes through."

"I helped design the system. I worked for Security before I worked for you. I gave him a code that will temporarily disable the recording of that data."

"That's possible?"

Anthony smiled. "No. It just omits the entry from his station. He'll think he's safe."

"And he bought all of that?"

"No. I promised him a promotion and gave him a twenty for his trouble."

"You *bribed* him?"

"No. You did. I just haven't vouchered it yet."

Pierce slowly became aware of the fact that he was sitting in pitch dark on what he suspected was a stairwell. Reaching out, he found the wall and, carefully moving his hand upward, discovered a handrail.

A light would help. Seems like they should have emergency lights.

They? Who are they? Where am I?

I was standing in a stream, wide, pure, water gurgling and splashing through the rocks, glistening with the light of a warm mid-day sun, blue skies, puffy clouds, and fresh air.

I had a pole and was casting out into the water...,

Sounds of shuffling, some kind of movement came from further up the stairs. Pierce moved up against the wall, keeping one hand on the handrail and the other to deflect anything that might be coming down.

Silence, as each became aware of the other.

"Hello?" Pierce whispered. "Who's there?"

"It's me..., Joseph. That you, Pierce?"

"Who else would it be? I think we're back in the stairwell."

"I was in Japan, downtown Tokyo, I think. Night time, lights flashing, people everywhere. Must've been a Friday or Saturday night, the way everyone was drinking. What *happened*?"

"Malcolm's cloud. That's what that was. I was fishing on a stream in what I think was Montana. I had felt soled boots so I wouldn't slip on the rocks, and I had a six weight, eight and a half foot long fishing pole. What the hell does that *mean*? I've never been fishing in my whole life! We're in the stairwell."

"Some guy stuck money into my bra and felt me

146

up. I was a stripper in a nightclub. I was a woman! Jesus."

"I don't want to hear it. That's something you'll have to work out later with your psychiatrist." Pierce cautiously stood and began working his way back up the steps. "Let's go see what kind of damage has been done."

"Bras are not very comfortable," said Joseph, slowly standing, hanging onto the rail. "The nerve of that guy! Did he really think I'd let him take advantage of me for just a few yen?"

"Shut up, Joseph."

Coming out of the door, they squinted into the light as building power came back on. Lights were humming overhead. Messages were coming in from everywhere, words flashing across screens, communication lines buzzing.

Stepping over the broken glass, Pierce made his way back to his office, to his balcony, and looked out over the grounds below.

People were running everywhere. Others, for whatever reasons, sitting on the benches or just standing there, looking stunned.

Pierce found himself yearning for a simpler life. Hearing all of the calls coming in, unanswered, sirens going off, seeing the chaos below, more than anything else in the world, he wanted to find that stream, breathe that air and get his line out in the water.

I want to feel the tug of a rainbow trout hitting my line. I want to gut it, skin it, build a fire under my frying pan, smell the butter melting while I bread the fish.

And I want to drink a long cold beer while I watch it cook in the pan.

What happened? When did life inside a dome be-

come more important than living?

I don't like this place. Pay's not that good.

Hmm. Wonder if I can find that stream.

He did not ask Joseph what he was longing for.

Mandy

Joseph stopped mid-sentence when he saw Mandy come through the double doors. Out in the hallway, seeing her approach the room, being careful to step over the broken glass in her high heel shoes, it had appeared that she was wearing either a very short skirt, or short shorts.

But coming through the doors, he saw that she was not wearing any pants at all, only her bikini style, semi-see-through white silk panties, and a red blouse.

"Um, sir? We have a visitor."

"What now?" Pierce whirled around in his chair, ready to yell at whoever it was, hoping that it was Malcolm. But when he saw Mandy, his jaw dropped and he fell silent.

"Um," he said, calmly. "May I help you?"

"Yeah. I'd like to, like, report a crime."

Pierce leaned back in his chair and studied her. This would be a very sexy woman anyway, with her slight build, fresh creamy skin and long dark hair. She had high cheekbones and looked like she'd have dimples if she smiled, which she was not. Without pants, she was beautiful.

"What type of crime?"

"Like..., hello! I lost my pants! I was just like, walking, and then this..., like a cloud somehow landed on me and like, took my pants. Whose cloud is that? Because I'm going to, like..., sue."

"You'll have to, like, get in line," said Pierce, suppressing a smile. "How did you, like, get past security downstairs?"

"Like..., hello! A woman without pants can go, like, wherever she wants. There must be like, twenty guys

149

downstairs following me around. Your guard like, stopped them at the door. I need some pants. And I want to, like, file a complaint. What was that thing, anyway? It's like nothing I've ever seen."

"What's your name?" said Pierce, bringing up the 'Reports' screen. He hadn't taken a report in five years. But this one he'd handle personally.

"Mandy - Laurence - Olivia - Rodriguez."

"I don't have that much room in the box. Pick any three. Joseph. Quit gawking and go get Mandy a blanket out of the emergency room."

"Right now, sir?"

"Of course, right now. Would you like to sit down, Mrs.? Miss Rodriguez? May I get you some coffee?"

"Coffee? Hello! You got a bottle of like, hard stuff? I'm sure you've got something in that drawer there."

Pierce smiled. "You're right. Coffee would only excite us more. As you can see, I'm like, having a bad hair day as well. Yes. Scotch, it is. I don't know if we have any, like, ice."

"Just like, hand me the bottle."

Joseph returned with the blanket as Mandy was taking a long swig. She looked over at him, glanced around the room, taking it all in for the first time, took another long swig, and then handed Joseph the bottle in exchange for the blanket.

"So, this is like, where it all happens, huh?"

Pierce laughed. "Yes. Especially, like, today. Hand me that bottle Joseph."

Joseph took a long swig and, coughing, handed it over.

"I was, like, walking up South Street," said Mandy. "And I was like, right there at the Inner Plaza when it started like, getting dark, and I was, like, wondering why it was getting dark in the morning. I mean, like, I've seen some pretty big clouds come over the

150

dome during, like, storms and stuff, but the dome lights usually, like, come on, so you don't, like, notice when that happens. But this time, it just, like, got dark. Next thing I know, I feel, like I'm not here anymore, like I went someplace else. You know what I mean? And when I came back, I had like, no pants."

Pierce had gotten up, walked over to the counter and fetched three cups. He returned to his desk, set them out and poured three more stiff shots. "I know, like, exactly what you mean."

And he now wanted to include Mandy in his quest to find that sparkling stream out under clear blue skies and fresh air. "Let's get the form filled out, so we can, like, move on. Mrs., or Miss?"

Tess looked at the translucent, golden glow of what would normally be her arm, made a fist of her right hand and then her left, watching how the energy flowed with the movement. And then she opened both hands wide and waved them in front of her face, crossing one hand in front of the other, fascinated by the play of light.

Ramon did not appear as fluid. His material let less light pass through and he was less fluid with his movements. But the paths of energy flowing throughout his body were far more complex than what Tess saw in hers.

"Those androids. What were their names?"

Ramon seemed startled by her words. "Jackson and Jeanette, Miss Tess."

"Would they have tried to take us prisoners?"

"My predictions were, yes. But we could not have allowed that."

"What would you do to stop them?"

"It is unclear whether my jamming capabilities would work on them since I did not have occasion to use it. It may not work on technology that is one hundred years superior to ours. It would have been our first source of resistance."

"And if that failed?"

"I have what Jordan terms, 'the frequilizer.' I scan all potential sources of danger and determine their resonant frequency, what holds them together and load a program that directs a transmitter back at them capable of breaking them apart. I had already analyzed both of them and was ready to use it. The problem is, if I attempt to use one of our weapons, what kind of defense, or offense, would it activate from their side? The situation could deteriorate very quickly."

"What if they took us prisoners?"

"It is not possible, Miss Tess. If the probe was opened, we would have been annihilated."

"Why?"

"It is only my prediction. If, in their world, the probe had already been annihilated, which it was because the side of the mountain was gone, then that energy had already dissipated, taking us with it. Opening the probe would cause an imbalance in that reality and we would be absorbed."

"Into what?"

"Their world. We would turn into nothing because we were already gone."

"This is hopeless, Ramon. What are we doing out here?"

"Actually, Miss Tess, my curiosity programming is having a field day, as Jordan would say. We have learned that one reality, one hundred years out from our launch date, contained a catastrophe that included us. Since we know that that scenario is not true, we have learned which path not to take. We now have two points in time and space that exist, our launch and the one that we just visited. And that gives us two perspectives from which to calculate our next move."

"What the hell was I thinking when I agreed to this? I never thought I was crazy before I had a robot! Ramon, you are not good for me. Take me back. I'll take the polluted air and water, find myself somebody, buy a case of wine and live. I don't need all of this."

"Miss Tess, we are on the brink of the most important discovery of humankind. If we understand how to navigate through time, the next step is how to navigate through space during that time, which, in the case of this probe, all it needs is propulsion. And if we are already pure energy, propulsion is just a matter of charge, shifting energy from one side of the craft to another to propel us in the direction that we want to go. We can travel at the speed of light. When we return back to the launch site, with your permission and at great expense to them, I will initiate changes to the navigational system. Currently, their programming is exceedingly primitive compared to what we now know."

"What you know. I don't know any of this."

"Incorrect, Miss Tess. My knowledge is your knowledge. And only you and Jordan have access to it. I am currently calculating our next destination to a time that existed minutes before Jordan disappeared. It is important to know what condition Eclipse was in before it launched."

"That's not what I told you to do. I said, go back. I'm done."

"Miss Tess...,"

"No."

"Do you know that he almost quit his job, rather than leave you?"

"What are you talking about?"

"Jordan. He was given orders to become Lindy Moore's lover and spy on her."

"Why are you telling me this? To make me change my mind?"

"No, Miss Tess. And, per your instructions, I am currently readjusting our destination back to the launch site, in real time. I will notify you when that task is complete."

"Thank you. Why is it that this probe is working and Malcolm's is not?"

"I predict that Cond-Orbit's probe is working but has lost communication. It is the inability of the homing devices to connect. The programming on this craft appears to be working properly."

"Why didn't Jordan take you with him? If you were there, you'd know how to override the controls and input the correct readings."

"Miss Tess. Jordan knows his craft. I suspect that I would have been given incorrect homing information, as well. I suspect sabotage."

"You didn't answer my question. Why didn't he take you? Surely he knew your value."

"He wanted me to protect you."

Tess started crying, not that it actually was crying, rather, a feeling of darkness rolling down what would be her cheeks, leaving little trails of dark energy shadows behind. How long ago it seemed that he had held her close, that she could hear his breathing, feel his gentle touch and laugh at his arrogant smile. "How much longer does he have?"

"Twenty-one hours, approximately. I have computed our return journey, Miss Tess. When you are ready, please...,"

"What will happen to him?"

"I predict that he will be annihilated. The energy levels and composite frequencies of both the craft and the stand must be the same. If he lands anywhere else, there will be a discharge of energy from one reality to the other. A human would not be able to withstand the through-rush of energy."

"He'll be electrocuted?"

"Vaporized, is a word that better describes the event."

"Will he feel pain?"

"I predict that he will not, Miss Tess. He won't have time to process it."

"Ramon, what is the meaning of all of this?"

"I do not understand your question, Miss Tess."

"Us humans. We're born. We run around for a while doing things. We die. What's the point?"

"Miss Tess. It would help if you understood that the human species, as a whole, is a collective consciousness. What you and Jordan are doing is the new apex of human understanding. Whether or not you succeed, you will be in all of the history books from this time forward."

"I hadn't thought of it like that. So..., if we go back without exhausting all possibilities for finding Jordan, that will all be recorded, won't it?"

"I predict that that is true."

"I'll be known forever as the selfish old bitch who gave up on Jordan to save her own skin."

"They will search for the facts, Miss Tess."

"Damn you, Jordan! Sucked me right in. Ramon?"

"Yes, Miss Tess?"

"How long would it take you to make changes to go to Jordan's pre-launch time?"

"Approximately five of our minutes, Miss Tess."

"Make the changes."

"Yes, Miss Tess."

"How come you don't argue when I tell you to do something that you want?"

"I only question your decisions when they are counter to your logic, Miss Tess."

"You sound just like Jordan. It's frightening."

"Miss Tess, have you considered what you will say to Jordan, should we be able to connect with him?"

"I thought it was just coordinates. You know, numbers, positions, that kind of thing. What are you proposing, Ramon?"

"You may never have the opportunity to speak with this man again. What things do you want to say?"

The lights to Malcolm's office flicked on automatically as he and Anthony entered the room. Malcolm headed for the coffee pot and started making a fresh pot. "Still haven't heard anything from Lindy. We need to hear from Tess. And we've got to get hold of Pierce. He's going to give us an earful. I really don't like how this day is going." Then he turned back to Anthony with an irritated look. "Tell me, what do you think Lindy's going to want out of all of this?"

"I suspect she'll want half."

"Half? We did all of the work, the testing...,"

"She has a system that appears to be working while yours is not. There's a lot to be said for that, Malcolm."

"We have the patents."

"No. You have patents pending. I did a little research and discovered that some of the more controversial ideas have not yet been applied for. I'm guessing that Cond-Orbit, not you personally, is not sharing this information with the U. S. Government because it's not legal for them to be doing what they're doing. And then I discovered that some of these ideas have patents pending under Lindy's company name. Apparently, she took some risks that Cond-Orbit chose not to."

"Why didn't you tell me this before we went there?"

"Because you were more worried about Tess. Maybe I should have stayed there. At least I could be helping to contact her."

"And what would you do that Lindy's not already doing. What's going on with you two? You're awfully friendly, it seems."

"We've always worked well together. Business interests aside, she's a fun person to be around."

"What does that mean?"

"It means, Malcolm, that I am paid by Cond-Orbit to do a job to the best of my ability, to make sure this project's a success and I will do whatever it takes to make it happen. And..., it's also in my best interest. Now, as far as Lindy goes, if I can glean anything from her or her operation, I will. And it will be Cond-Orbit's gain. That's what I'm paid to do."

"Here comes a call."

Dorian Zimmer's face popped up on the monitor. He was wearing a beret and had grown a goatee. "Hey, Malcolm. Look's like the party's heating up down there. Anything I can do to help?"

Malcolm managed a nervous laugh. "Yeah. Shoot me, if you've got a gun that'll hit its target three hundred miles away."

"Don't miss," said Anthony. "I'm standing right next to him. I'm Anthony Swincer, by the way."

"Hi, Anthony. I'm Dorian Zimmer. Are you going to get things under control for Malcolm?"

"Working on it."

"Malcolm, I called because, ever since our last talk, I've been studying your dome with some state of the art equipment. From up here, I can tell where your probe is. Not all of the time. But when it attempts a return, I can detect where it is long before you."

"Can you get us that information in real time?"

"Of course, I can. What will you do with it?"

"At least we could clear the area."

"I've heard," said Dorian, "that Security is issuing orders to clear the dome. Is that correct?"

"Yeah," said Malcolm, with a sigh. "Pierce, in Operations, covering his butt. I can't control that. He doesn't want to get caught in the middle of all...,"

"The reason I say this," Dorian interrupted, "is that

the secrecy of this project is now out the window. Rather, out the dome. How are you going to contain this, Malcolm? There are going to be lots of questions."

"We don't know how it's going to play out yet. We'll have to wait and see."

"The folks up here aren't liking what's going on."

"Well..., I asked for some direction on how to proceed, early on. They never got back to me."

Dorian leaned back in his chair and studied Malcolm and Anthony. "Up here, I have certain advantages that you don't. I get to mingle with these folks. We have dinners together. They're good people, you'd like them, but they're ruthless. As soon as it was confirmed that the probe disappeared, they started an investigation. They have a lot of money in this and they're going to protect it. The way I see it coming down, literally, is that you were running an illegal operation inside the dome against all company policies."

"What? You've got to be kidding. The accounting trail alone will prove that...,"

"What accounting trail? Malcolm, I tell you because I like you. You try hard and I think you're a good man. There will be no trail."

"When can you get us that information on the probe's location?" Anthony asked, trying to change the subject.

"It's coming at you now on thirty-seven," said Dorian. "And since we're on the subject, we set up extra surveillance on your dome. It took us a while to figure out what we were seeing, but now that we know that it's associated with the probe, we're getting some valuable information."

"What kind of detectors?" said Anthony, holding his pencil ready.

Dorian smiled. "Wouldn't you like to know? And this brings me to the next item on my list. While calibrating our detectors, we noticed a second force, about eighty miles west of the dome that had the same kind of energy. We've just tracked the two of you traveling out to that location and back while the dome was under siege. I have to ask, why?"

Malcolm had this sinking feeling in his gut that the trap had just been set. "That's correct. We'd heard that they had something similar over there. We went to see for ourselves."

"And, does it work?"

"It appears to," said Anthony.

"Question is, why is their probe working and Cond-Orbit's probe is not?"

"That's exactly what we're trying to find out," said Malcolm.

"The answer might be sitting right next to you, Malcolm. Anthony has been out to that location before."

"What?"

"I was abducted," said Anthony. "I had nothing to do with that. I insisted that I would not help in any way and implored them to let me go."

"And they did," said Dorian, calmly. "You moved straight into Lindy's old condo inside the dome. How convenient."

"That was legal. And it had nothing to do with Lindy. I rented it through an agency."

"Ah, Lindy. Why is it that her name keeps popping up?"

"OK," said Anthony, holding up his hands. "I know it looks suspicious to both of you. I am not employed by that operation, not serving that operation in any way except by Malcolm's and my agreed actions. I have no affiliation with them."

Malcolm had been watching Anthony squirm in his

chair. Not that he was squirming, more like nervous fidgets, tapping his pencil on his note pad, rubbing his nose as if he had an itch, running his hands through his hair. "Why didn't you tell me that you had been abducted?"

"There hasn't been time. We've been working on getting this...,"

"You did make time to meet with Lindy," said Dorian. "Over coffee, since she left the dome."

"Her condo was sacked. I packed her stuff up, put it into storage and gave her the key. That's all."

Malcolm's face was slowly becoming as red as his hair. "Jesus, Anthony! Why didn't you talk to me? All this time..., and you just kept mum?"

"Malcolm, it hasn't affected anything that we've done. You and I are trying to solve this problem and none of this stuff has any bearing on what we're attempting to do."

"Well," said Dorian, with a sigh. "Just wanted to give you a heads-up, Malcolm. I don't know whether Anthony is your lifesaver or your anchor. That's for you to decide. You have a lot of other good people working on this project. Keep them in mind."

"Thanks, Dorian."

"Good luck."

Pierce was having trouble concentrating. Mandy had passed out on his couch and he had to go over there more than once and put her blanket back on. She tossed and turned a lot, was very exciting to watch, but he had a job to do.

He brought up the screen associated with the telescope on the north side of the building, pointed it west and upped the magnification until Zodi's truck came into view. He didn't have enough power to bring in Zodi's and Anthony's faces clearly, but the vehicle image was reasonably sharp.

"Malcolm? You on here?"

"I'm here."

"I'm sending you live data. You've got the truck on your screen?"

"Got it."

"Anthony. Can you hear me?"

"Yeah. I'm here."

Pierce rubbed his temples, opened his desk drawer, retrieved two aspirin from a little green plastic bottle, tossed one into his mouth, followed it with a large gulp of water and repeated the process. He cleared his throat.

"OK. Talk to me. What is this thing, Malcolm?"

"I'm not sure."

"Right. That's the answer I expected. Zodi?"

"Yeah, Boss?"

"Your truck is running OK? It's got a full charge?"

"Right. I can probably go six more hours on this charge."

Pierce leaned back in his chair. "Malcolm, my first question is, how do you know where it is when it's invisible?"

"It's being tracked from our headquarters, in orbit."

"So..., they know about it as well. What are they calling it?"

"It's classified, Pierce. Give it up. Let's just call it a cloud."

"A cloud, it is. OK, Anthony. Where are you in relation to it?"

"Looks like it's about a quarter mile away, up near the top of the dome. Zodi and I will...,"

"God willing!" Zodi yelled.

"Zodi and I will park beneath it, prepare the signal generators for launch and wait for the probe to...,"

"Probe?" Pierce leaned forward in his chair. "What kind of probe?"

"You don't have a need to know," said Malcolm. "Let's just keep calling it a cloud."

"It's a stairway to Heaven," Zodi volunteered. "I was there!"

Zodi gladly volunteered to assist Anthony with the project. And she had never reported into the hospital as Pierce had instructed. Rather, she headed straight for Shepard's Choice Church, located two blocks northeast of the Main Plaza, walked straight through the front doors, threw a month's worth of pay into the donations box, went straight to the front of the church, kneeled down and began to pray. No matter that there was a wedding going on at the time. News of her story spread like wildfire.

Mandy turned to her other side, exposing one of her long, slim legs and just a tiny bit of her underwear. Pierce was glad that he had her in the room all to himself. Joseph didn't want to go, but Pierce had insisted that he head up the emergency crew down at the fire station.

And he thought of that sparkling stream again,

imagined the raw, unfiltered sun on his back, imagined the heat it would generate without the dome in between and marveled at how much power the current had as the water splashed through the rocks. He would have to stay close to Mandy, make sure that she didn't get carried away.

How soon can I make that happen? She's divorced. How wonderful is that? I wonder if she knows how to cook. Humph. Doesn't matter.

"We're directly below it," said Anthony. "Zodi? Pull over, and let's get these things ready."

"Looks like I'm starting to see some action up there," said Pierce, watching the monitor. "Malcolm, you see that, too?"

"I do. Looks like it just materializes. Is that what I'm seeing?"

"That's what it does," said Pierce. "From my experience, it displaces the reality that we are in and substitutes it for something else."

"Is that what you felt?"

"It's what I saw, something like," and here Pierce smiled, thinking of how Mandy talked, "like the stuff that makes up my world just, like, disappears. I found myself in another place...,"

"Heaven!" Zodi yelled, cheerfully.

"It wasn't hell," said Pierce. "But I imagine that for some people, it could be the most terrifying thing they've ever seen. I'm expecting heart attacks if it hits the general population. Here it comes. Anthony? Getting dark over there?"

"Holy crap, yes! Zodi? Don't activate the release until you've locked the snap connector in place because it can..., God damn it! What did I say?"

"Nice," said Pierce. "Looks like the balloon is going up without the signal generator."

"Send the other one," said Malcolm. "At least get

one up there."

"Doing that now," said Anthony. "Gone. Pray for it to work."

"What, exactly is that thing going to do?" said Pierce.

"We're attempting to establish communications," Malcolm replied. "Anthony, you've got another spare and a whole tank of helium. See if you can get it launched."

"Getting pretty dark," said Anthony, as he began connecting up all the parts. "Takes a while to fill the balloon."

"Looks like it's drifting lower," said Pierce. "You two might want to get out of there and do the balloon thing later."

"Good idea," said Anthony. "But now I've got a half-filled balloon. That's not going to travel well in a moving truck."

"Praise the Lord!" Zodi yelled, holding her arms open. "It's alive! Look at all of that power! See how the light turns on and off and how it just..., appears. It's..., glorious!"

"Anthony? Get your butt out of there," said Malcolm. "Just tie the balloon down to the bed of the truck and move. Pierce is right. It's better to have a spare for later."

"We agree on something," said Pierce. "Zodi? Get in the truck and get out of there."

"Getting dark," said Anthony. "Zodi? If you don't move, I'm going to leave you here. Now, get in the fricking truck, turn the key and let's go!"

With all of the commotion going on, Mandy woke up. She looked around the room for a while, trying to figure out where she was, looked over at Pierce, sitting at his desk and very much involved in some event unfolding on the monitor, and moaned.

"Oh…, my God! I thought it was, like, a dream!"

Pierce looked over at her, smiled, and returned his attention to the screen. "Looks like it's heading east. Anthony? You're going to get in front of it?"

"Yep, doing that now. Zodi? Floor it. Let's get ahead of this thing."

Mandy got up, wrapped the blanket around her, went over and stood behind Pierce, looking at the screen and let out a gasp. "That's, like, the cloud!"

"It is," Pierce replied. "We're tracking it, trying to communicate with it."

"It has, like, intelligence?" Mandy asked. "What is it?"

"No idea," said Pierce, hoping that Mandy would forget about the blanket and let it fall open.

"Who is that with you?" Malcolm asked. "This is a confidential operation."

Pierce managed a short smile at the thought of it. "Confidential went out the window a couple of days ago."

"How are you going to, like, communicate with a cloud?" Mandy asked.

"You need to get her out of there," said Malcolm. "Unless she's assigned to Security in some way, and it looks like she isn't, standing around in a blanket. What the hell is she doing there anyway?"

"This is one of your victims, Malcolm. Say hello to Mandy."

"That's like, *your* cloud?" said Mandy, voice rising. She flung her blanket open, exposing herself to the camera. "See that, Malcolm! I have, like, no pants. Lost them in the cloud! I'm going to, like, sue for hostage taking, and like, defamation of character, and like, emotional stress. When I'm done with you, Malcolm, you're going to have, like, no clothes. Because I'm, like, taking everything."

166

Pierce burst out laughing.

"First we've got to stop it," said Anthony. "Zodi? Pull over at the next intersection and we'll launch from there."

"Don't think you're going to have time," said Pierce. "Looks like it's coming down."

Mandy leaned over Pierce's shoulder to get a better look. "Like, where is that thing?"

"West of us," said Pierce, looking up and taking in the essence of her perfume.

"Is it, like, coming at us?"

"It's still, like, pretty far away," said Pierce, trying not to notice that Mandy's blanket was still open.

She took note of that, pulled the blanket around her and headed for the coffee pot. "Like, you're Pierce, right?"

"Right."

"You got, like…, any food around here? Cause I'm, like, starving."

"Can you cook?" Pierce asked, actually wanting to know the answer to that question more than what was happening inside the dome.

"Holy crap!" Anthony yelled. "It's coming down fast!"

"Praise the Lord!" Zodi screamed.

Anthony grabbed the frame of the window, pulled himself out of the truck far enough so that he could get a good look up at the cloud. "Doesn't this thing go any faster?"

"Nope," said Zodi. "It caught me last time."

"Turn left at the next intersection."

"That'll take us toward Center."

Anthony pulled himself back in and reconnected his seat belt. "I want to see if we can lose it."

"Maybe," said Zodi, with a smile. "Maybe not. Follows me everywhere. Something about these tires."

"Turn, turn, turn! OK. Punch it! Let's go!"

They skidded around the corner and Zodi floored it, not that the truck had much speed or that it burned rubber. Peeling out of the curve? Nope, none of that. It did skid around the corner and then lurch forward.

"Jesus." said Anthony, shaking his head. "Why did you pick this vehicle?"

"You said you wanted to make contact with the cloud."

"But I don't want to mingle with it!"

"Pierce doesn't want me to head toward Center when the cloud's chasing me."

"What?"

"He doesn't want it going into the crowded areas."

"What crowded areas? Everybody's leaving." Anthony released his seat belt, stuck his head out the window. "It's getting closer."

"That's what happened last time. When it gets real close, all the electrical goes haywire on the truck and then we'll come to a rolling stop. Praise the Lord."

"You're sure of this?"

"Why do you think I volunteered?"

"I have an idea. Pull over."

"Here?"

"Yes. That last signal generators is in the truck. All we have to do is activate it and get away from the truck. Stop, stop, stop. Let's make a run for it, that building over there."

As the truck skidded to a halt, Anthony flung the door open, reached into the bed of the truck, flipped the switch to activate the transmitter and then turned and raced for the concrete block building. He had gone about fifty feet when he turned around, looking for Zodi, and saw her still rummaging through some equipment in the bed of the truck.

"What are you doing? Come on!"

She picked up the signal generator, wrapped her arms around it, held it close and smiled. "I'm going to make sure He gets the message."

"What are you, crazy?"

"I've been running around my whole life doing nothing. I want to stop and believe in something."

"Zodi. That cloud is not what you think it is. It's a high-energy probe, looking for a place to land. And when it does, it's gonna go boom. Now..., come on. If the cloud finds the truck, it'll find the signal generator. There's no need for you to go with it. Come with me."

"I've been in that..., cloud, as you call it. You have no idea what it feels like to be in the presence of The Lord. I will go there again, a million times out of a million."

"What you saw was the beginning of death! If the probe had actually made that leap back, there would have been a huge explosion. It's piloted by a human..., and he pulled back from landing because he knew it wasn't going to work."

"And this time it will," said Zodi, with a smile.

Anthony turned and headed for the building. "Suit yourself. Good luck, Zodi."

The air crackled as the cloud approached ground, hovering at about one hundred feet, bursts of light and shades of shadows, pulsing on and off, bits of a new reality spitting out, looking for a place to become something over here.

"Praise the Lord!" Zodi screamed triumphantly as she lifted her arms outward.

First Clue

Malcolm put the call up on the screen. Stella looked up from her stack of papers, smiled at Malcolm and then reached for her tea. "Hi, Malcolm," she said cheerfully. "Looks like you've stirred up that hornet's nest that you were talking about. Is there anything I can do to help?"

"Save yourself," said Malcolm, looking very worried. "We've got a couple more tricks that we can try but I'm not hopeful."

"Still can't locate the probe?"

"We can tell where it is. We're attempting to send it homing information."

"Do you expect to talk with Jordan?"

"Probably not."

"Malcolm, Angel has provided me with some information that might be useful. Do you remember Angel?"

"Ah, yes. Your communications spy. What has she got to say?"

"She hasn't deciphered all of it yet. She claims that she has communicated with a robot named Ramon. Do you know of Ramon?"

"Of course, I do. He belongs to Tess. What about him?"

"He and Angel discovered each other while engaging in, shall we call it, anonymous searches for information?"

"I did not know he had that kind of capability."

"Apparently he has many talents. Angel received a message from him, time stamped almost one hundred years from now."

"What?"

"Angel can translate every known form of communication but the code in which this has been received hasn't been invented yet. It appears that, at some time in the future, they changed how they process information. So, my question is, how was he able to do that?"

"Stella, I've been so busy, I haven't had time to give you a call. There was a second craft that was built."

"I see."

"You remember Lindy?"

"Of course, I do."

"Well, she's duplicated our efforts."

"How was that even possible?"

"An international conglomerate with lots of money can pretty much do whatever it wants."

"Never did like her. Too catty."

"Tess is in that vehicle with Ramon."

"What? Wait. Let me think this through. So, does that mean it's…, working? That call from the future is legitimate?"

"It might be."

"My, God, Malcolm. I think I'm speechless. Do you understand what this means? Life, as we know it, is going to end."

"I think mine is going to end sooner than that if I can't get that probe back on the stand. I'm crunched for time and I need to give this information to Anthony."

"There is another reason that I called. Did you know that Anthony and Lindy met over coffee the other day?"

"Yeah. I just heard about it."

"You trust him?"

"I wish I could go into the future and find out. Thanks, Stella."

"Good luck, Malcolm."

"Eclipse calling Cond-Orbit. Come in. I am not picking up your tracking signal. Both my primary and back-up receivers test OK. I am transmitting across all of the emergency channels. Do you read me? I will attempt another landing when the probe is back up to full power. This is Eclipse calling Cond-Orbit. Anybody read me?"

A red light located in the bottom left of his dashboard flashed on and off, an alarm indicating a power drain. Jordan reset the alarm. When it reappeared, he queried the logic controller and requested a test of the power program. Normal.

The light blinked off, flickered once or twice and then came back on, this time to stay. Jordan waited for the emergency power to kick in and when it didn't, selected Manual Override.

The screen came to life long enough to tell him that excessive heat was being detected in the aft power compartment and that preventative measures were being implemented.

When Jordan attempted to get more information, that screen went blank. Cockpit lighting was the next to go and Jordan found himself sitting in the dark.

"Eclipse to Cond-Orbit. Anybody home? Got some problems here. Looks like I've lost control power. Eclipse to Cond-Orbit. Come in?"

Still have air. Wonder how long that will last.

"This is Eclipse. Anybody read me?"

Should've built the probe for easier maintenance. I could've crawled back there and seen what the problem was.

But..., no. That would've doubled the cost. Probe

173

would've had to be wider, used more material, need-ed more power, would've been costlier to launch.

They don't have to get in it.

Hmm. Wonder if I have transmit power. Could be, I just slowly and quietly wait for my time to be up. I'll disappear into nothingness.

Wonder what that feels like.

"Eclipse to Cond-Orbit. Anybody read me? I have lost instrument power and might be forced to make an emergency landing. This is Jordan Blake in Eclipse. Anybody read me?"

Well, Malcolm. It was a good ride. I know that we're on to something. It works. It's just that this first one won't work. But you'll learn from it. I'll go down in history..., should make someone a lot of money.

"This is Eclipse to Cond-Orbit. I am flying blind. I have no instrumentation. The craft is overheating. I cannot determine the source of the problem and I don't know how much longer I will have air. I'm go-ing to attempt to land. This is Eclipse to Cond-Orbit. Anybody read me?"

"Miss Tess, with your permission, I will activate the settings that will take us to one hour before Jordan launched his probe. If both of these probes are built exactly the same, as we are led to believe, that one should also be functioning at that time. It would be to our advantage to compare the database of Jordan's probe to this one."

"How are you going to do that?"

"Miss Tess, because of my ability to communicate with Cond-Orbit, I can use that link to our advantage. Jordan has provided the necessary passwords for me to access the database of the probe."

"How are you going to go back to the time when Jordan launched? We hadn't even launched, yet."

"Miss Tess, if we are on a time continuum, then we can choose to enter any reality that links to it. We will travel to Jordan's pre-launch...,"

"How can you *do* that?"

"I am beginning to understand that problems that humans have concerning time travel. Perhaps it would help you to understand that if everything is connected, then it does not matter when we launch this probe, only that at some point in time we get into it and launch."

"Physically, we're not really traveling anywhere, right?"

"That is correct, Miss Tess. We have never left the launch stand. We do not have the ability to physically change our location but that can be corrected upon our return."

"Let's hope that's possible. All right, Ramon. Go for it. I'm already stuck out here. I'm not cut out for it and I want it to be done."

"We have arrived, Miss Tess."

"I just now gave the OK."

"I had already pre-calculated that destination. It takes no time to get there."

Tess watched as the shapes of their own launch pad slowly came back into view outside her window, not a clear image. Rather, more like a translucent picture of the place. She could see technicians walking around taking measurements, a man and a woman standing in one corner of the room, with their white coats and clipboards, having a conversation.

"Miss Tess, we are an overlay of Lindy's craft, the one that is here one hour before Jordan launches. They cannot see us. I am attempting to connect into the database of Jordan's probe at this time."

"So..., Jordan's probably walking around inside Cond-Orbit's lab, checking things, making sure everything's ready to go."

"I am connected into the link, waiting for clearance into the project, Miss Tess."

"If I am here with you now, where am I in that world?"

"At this time, in that reality, you were not at the house. You had taken an IDT to San Diego, missed your connection and wound up in Dome Chula Vista. This is what you told me that night. Or, put another way, if we were in that reality, that is what you will tell me tonight, when you come home."

"I remember. That's when I bought that lamp."

"That is correct. It is approximately one-thirty in the afternoon, in that reality."

"That's when I was getting into the IDT, heading back up to LA."

A bell rang and the doors to the car closed. Haltingly, Tess found a seat and plopped down before she fell as the car lurched forward.

"You OK, miss?"

A stranger's voice, coming out of thin air.

"Wha..., what?"

"Are you OK? You look faint. I'm a doctor."

Looking up, Tess saw the face of a young man, clean-shaven, with brown eyes and a tussle of black hair. His face was familiar. She knew him from somewhere but couldn't remember when.

People were staring, the woman in the red coat sitting across the isle, a man in a gray suit, wearing wire-rimmed glasses, looking over the top of his paper, a couple of teenagers who were probably cutting class, all of them she'd seen before.

"Are you OK? I'm a doctor. Do you need help?"

"I..., I'm fine. Thank you."

And then came a wave of dizziness, confusion from being in two places at the same time...,

"Miss Tess, I recommend that you do not dwell too strongly on your life in that time. It can be confusing for humans to have too many inputs. You are here in the probe, with me. For us, that time has already passed."

"I haven't even looked at that lamp since I bought it."

"That is correct, Miss Tess. And, in that reality, the lamp will arrive at the house later tonight."

It seemed so long ago, the lamp. Who would ever think to make a lamp like that? And why did it feel so good to think of touching something tangible, feeling the cold bronze faces, the smooth marble base, seeing the soft glow of the crystal and feeling the warmth of the light? How far away that seemed now. Life was so simple..., only a few days ago. Tess started to cry.

"Miss Tess, you are wasting energy."

"Stuff it."

"I do not understand that phrase, Miss Tess."

"It means, shut up and mind your own business. I'm human. I'm allowed my feelings."

"I should categorize that phrase in the derogatory file?"

"That would be correct, Ramon."

"I have accessed the database and am analyzing the contents. I will advise when this task is complete."

"How long will that take?"

"I am running a comparator program. It should be complete within a few minutes, Miss Tess."

"How much longer does he have?"

"I have been doing an analyses of the survival programming and have determined that the seven days survival rating is based on optimum conditions. But I suspect that Jordan is having anything but optimum conditions because he is not able to land his craft. It could be...,"

"Get to the point."

"I suspect that Jordan may have four hours, more or less, depending on the damage to his craft from each attempt."

"Just like him. Never fall in love with a guy like that, Ramon. Not that you ever would."

"Miss Tess, perhaps you might consider telepathy. You are in the same time zone as Jordan, just before he launched. Talk to him."

"Hmm. What would I say?"

Well, Jordan..., butt head.

Gonna get us both killed, aren't you?

Thanks a lot. Nice to know I was loved.

Sitting in her cockpit, looking out at the lab, watching everyone doing things, waiting for Ramon to complete his task, a thought popped into her head.

Hey Tess, I love you, too.

"Miss Tess, I have completed the comparison of the databases and have determined that, at this point in time, that craft should be functional."

"You are sure?"

"Yes, Miss Tess."

"Then..., why is it failing?"

"May I suggest that we move forward in time, to the minutes just prior to his launch. It would help to know that the craft was functional at launch time. With your permission, I will make the adjustments."

"Do it."

The scene of their launch pad disappeared, and once again Tess found herself sitting in total darkness.

"This is the part I don't like, Ramon. I can't handle no input."

"As I gain knowledge, Miss Tess, these dark moments will shorten. I am currently readjusting the probe's display."

Slowly, light became visible and Tess found herself back in pure energy form, gazing at what would normally be her hands and arms. Instinctively, she moved her fingers, making sure that she still had control over the particles of light that comprised her body and discovering that the movement of them was effortless.

"Ramon? Do I need to breathe when I'm in this state?"

"The answer is both yes, and no, Miss Tess. Being human, you will always need to breath. But outside of time, as we are at this moment, no oxygen is required because we are in a pure energy state. Once we arrive into another reality, you will require oxygen again."

"Scary, but..., I think that made sense."

The hazy translucent image of their launch site

slowly reappeared. Lindy, talking to one of the technicians, suddenly turned and pointed up at the cockpit. Instinctively, Tess ducked down, feeling like a spy.

"They cannot see us, Miss Tess. All they see is an empty probe. I am reconnecting into the Cond-Orbit link."

"Jordan would be in the probe now?"

"I will be able to give specifics in just a few moments, Miss Tess."

"I thought I heard him, his voice, inside my head."

"At this moment?"

"No. At the end of our last..., what do I call it, journey?"

"I detected an increase in your heart rate and an uptake in your metabolic rate at that time, Miss Tess. I was going to question the reason for it if the opportunity came up."

"He said he loved me."

"That would be correct. He...,"

"Shut up, Ramon. Do your comparing."

"Yes, Miss Tess. I have tapped into the surveillance system utilized during Cond-Orbit's launch. On your monitor, you will see Jordan in the cockpit."

The camera's view of the probe was from the same perspective as that of Tess when she launched, aimed at the cockpit. Tess watched as Jordan checked his instruments, made sure his air supply was working, that the back-ups were functioning, the same things that she had been taught to do.

"There is one thing different in the database," said Ramon. "There is a new line of code that contains instructions to be implemented if the launch is successful. But I cannot determine what those instructions are because they won't be released unless the launch is successful."

"Can you tell who input it?"

"There are several persons authorized to input code. I can run a program that might identify the...,"

"They're powering up!"

A Sunny Day

The people remaining inside the dome, the ones who were going to fight the cloud, or at least attempt to resolve any issues or damage done by the cloud, definitely wanted the vending machines to stay powered up because who wants to do rescue work on an empty stomach?

And what real danger was there, anyway? No one had been killed or even hurt by the cloud. Mandy, it was now well known, had lost her pants but..., was that really such a bad thing? At this point, just about everyone had seen video of Mandy as she walked over to Security and disappeared inside.

Sales of panties like hers sold like hotcakes around the world.

And then there was Zodi. Rumors of her encounter with God spread like a brush fire ripping across the Plains. She had entered the cloud and not only survived, but saw the Truth of the Universe. She had heard the angels singing, been in the hands of The Lord and had been sent back to testify.

So, while the orders were to evacuate the dome, many were choosing to stay. Who better to be trapped inside the dome with, than The Lord?

Thinking along those same lines were the reporters, bloggers, twitters, tweeters, druggies that thought this would be a pretty cool event to see and maybe even better than the best drugs available. Why leave if you already have a front row seat?

In fact, what was really happening was that people outside the dome were now clamoring to get in. The guards secured all of the entrance gates in the mechanically locked position and then had to implement a one-at-a-time exit strategy for those still wanting to leave because people were attempting to come in through the exits.

Reporters from around the world flew into LA and rushed out to the dome. Video of Cond-Orbit's crowded entrances was communicated to the world and rumors sizzled with controversy, like melting butter in a too hot pan.

Temperatures outside the dome were in the nineties when the cloud reappeared a half mile west of the main power plant, a three story building that converted the high voltage power coming in from the solar cells down into something safer to use.

Power Central also kept the big fans turning, the blades that moved the air throughout the dome, and provided electricity to keep the dome's temperature under control, power the lights, computers and purify the air.

It also powered the pumps that moved the water throughout the dome and provided water pressure for all of the factories, businesses, private living quarters, and was used to cool the endless rows of power cells that were constantly in a state of charge or discharge.

Pierce, watching through his telescope and transmitting the data to Malcolm, sent word to shut down all non-essential power within the dome.

There was confusion as to what non-essential actually meant. Certainly, everyone agreed that the air supply was essential. Of course, running water was essential, which meant that the pumps had to be kept running. Shut down power to lighting? A lot of argument there. Essential lighting then, per the Emergency Plan? Only if you must. How about power to the computers, the real brains of the operation? No. Do not shut down the computers.

As a result, much of the power to the dome remained on and nothing much changed after the order to cut power. Power Central kept its breakers closed and all of the energy coming in from the solar cells on this very hot and sunny day, continued to flow down into the fuel cells.

"What I don't understand," said Pierce, glancing over at Malcolm's image, "is why the cloud is sometimes destructive and other times not."

"What was it with you?" Malcolm asked, wringing his hands nervously, something he'd been doing a lot of lately. He had also developed a nervous tick in his left eye and the lotion he'd been rubbing on his hands for the skin rash had now found a way up to his scalp, causing his hair to appear greasy.

"It displaced where I was, at least in my mind, because I don't think I was transported anywhere. But that's not the point. What I'm saying is that sometimes the cloud is conductive and sometimes it isn't."

"It, like, stole my pants," said Mandy, now munching on an energy bar that she'd discovered in the Emergency Supply room. Standing next to Pierce, she handed him one and watched the monitor. "Like..., how conductive is that? Tell me, Malcolm, where did they go?"

Before he could answer, the cloud engulfed the third floor of Power Central, lingered without incident for a moment, until the explosion, a fireball that blew out the windows with a loud boom, and then settled down into the remainder of the building, accompanied by several explosions.

All power to the Dome was suddenly cut off. The big fans slowly ground to a halt and, as they did, it became apparent that not only did they make a lot of noise, that low rumbling sound of the shafts turning inside their bearings day in and day out, but that they actually did move a lot of air. It did not take long for the dome to start heating up, like a lid on a pot getting ready to boil.

The computers were still running on back-up power, but all of the programs and instructions in the world were not going to keep the pumps running without power.

Without moving water, the heat exchangers could not transfer heat and the fuel cell temperatures began to rise. Without power, the dome became eerily silent, except for the sounds of everyone now stampeding for the exits.

"**M**iss Tess, I have to confess that I have information that I have not shared with you."

Tess let out a long sigh. She had just been thinking about, and relishing the idea of getting her life back. "What is it, Ramon?"

"During your absence, when you were abducted, I made accidental contact with a spy-bot named Angel. Since then, both Angel and I have been attempting to identify each other's positions and loyalties."

"Angel? Whom does she work for?"

"She is owned by a woman named Stella Powers, the employer of Drake Walker and Vivian Bustworthy."

"Ahh, yes. I had forgotten about them. Go on."

"Angel has been programmed to spy on all forms of communication. She is able to gain entry into links that deny me. Therefore, she is a useful tool. I have not yet determined that she shares your interests, just as she is analyzing us. But she has been a useful source of information."

"Ramon, get to the point."

"While you and the droids were conversing ninety-seven years from now, I sent a message to Angel containing our position and time. The droids spoke of two explosions on the same day. It is logical to assume...,"

"Wait. How did you know that Angel still existed?"

"I did not know, Miss Tess. But her digital address might still exist and if she is still able to process information as she does now, she might be able to read it."

"Why did you do that?"

"The droids spoke of two explosions on the same

186

day. If Jordan is unsuccessful in his attempt to land, then I suspect that we are tracking time in a reality that does not end well for us. My attempt to contact Angel was to facilitate our ability to update our knowledge in real time."

"And has that worked?"

"Yes, Miss Tess. Since then, Angel has volunteered confidential updated information of the events unfolding inside the dome."

"And now you're going to tell me something I can use."

"I regret to inform you, Miss Tess. But there has been an explosion inside Cond-Orbit."

"What? When? Is anyone hurt?"

"The explosion occurred approximately one hour ago, in real time. The dome has lost power and is heating up. Currently, the temperature inside the dome is one hundred and twenty-seven degrees, and rising."

"Everyone's evacuated?"

"No. Miss Tess. When dome power went out, power to the entrances and exits was cut, rendering them impassable. There are a few emergency exits, but they are overwhelmed with the rush of people. Angel reported that there are nearly seven hundred humans still trapped inside the dome."

"Jordan..., dead?"

"It is most likely, Miss Tess."

"Those people..., what will happen to them?"

"Miss Tess. In this reality, probability is that they will die. I suspect that we have to go back to the time between Jordan's launch and the time that he crashed, make an attempt to communicate and, if that is possible, make corrections to his probe's database."

"And leave these people to die?"

"You have no control over any of these realities, Miss Tess. Only which path you choose to take."

"How come you didn't tell me about Angel before?"

"It was my intent, Miss Tess. But events have been unfolding very quickly and my processing capabilities are at their limits. I am calculating our next time slot to be shortly after Jordan launched. I will attempt to correct the database of Jordan's probe. During that time, I suspect that you and Jordan will be able to communicate."

"I think I want a drink. A nice, dry martini. Make that a double, with lots of olives. Something that will knock my socks off."

"I do not know that phrase, Miss Tess."

"Makes me feel good, kind of numb."

"It is well known that insects prefer over-ripe fruit due to its alcohol content, especially those that are sex deprived. Numbing of the mind with alcohol feels good?"

"Yes, it does. Do it, Ramon. Let's get this over with."

Tess recoiled, first at the act of becoming it, and second at the thought of what she was actually doing, entering into the blink of an eye and becoming nothing.

She waited quietly for the light that she knew was coming, that dim glow that grew into something that she could perceive and then brighten to a color that she could identify, and eventually assume the shape of the cockpit, the launch stand and the dim silhouettes that made up the room, and her hands folded on her lap, twisted strands of light...,

Overload

Tess thought the words long before she realized that she had not actually heard them. She had been thinking about Jordan, about how innocent their time together had been at the beginning, like when they rented a cabin in Yosemite and hiked up to the top of Misty Falls. The falls were spectacular and, coming back down in the rain, they were wet, hungry and very much in love.

"Those were good times, weren't they, Tess?"

It took her a while to understand what had just happened, Jordan's voice ringing through her thoughts.

"Yes," she admitted, without saying anything. "They were the best."

"Let's do it again."

"You can't bring back the past."

"Let's start all over, you and me."

"There's too much between us. It'll never be the same."

"It'll be better."

"I wish that were true. But I don't trust you now."

"I'd prove you wrong if I had the chance."

"Of course, you would. Better than blowing yourself into eternity! What the hell is wrong with you?"

"We're on the cutting edge, Tess. You and me."

"The edge of death, more like. Jordan, grow up! Look at what is happening! People are dying because of your actions."

"What people?"

"Inside the dome. You're going to crash."

"How do you know this?"

"I've been there. You are going to die and take about seven hundred people with you."

"You time traveled?"

189

"Yes. We talked to two droids in the future. They...,"

"How did you time travel?"

"I don't know. Talk to Einstein here. Ramon? I'm sure that you're monitoring this conversation. Talk to the fool."

"Mr. Jordan. You are on a trajectory that will result in the death of several hundred humans inside the dome. We have determined that the database of your computer system has been contaminated."

"How did you time travel?"

"We do not have time for this conversation, Mr. Jordan. I recommend that...,"

"Just like you, Jordan. More worried about the project than the people."

"I do care. But this is the future. Tess, this is what we've been searching for!"

"No matter how many you kill to get it?"

"Mr. Jordan. Miss Tess. This is not helpful to the tasks at hand. Mr. Jordan, I recommend that I be given access to the probe's computer system."

"I personally checked that database. What's wrong with it?"

"There was a last minute set of instructions that stipulated that if the launch was successful, then the change to the database would take place."

"Lindy?"

"I suspect that that is true. However, it does not matter who made the change, only that we correct it. We do not have much time, Mr. Jordan."

"I knew it. Lindy. What a bitch."

"You were pretty excited about her when you left me."

"Work related, Tess. I had no choice."

"Bull pucky."

"It's always been you."

"Mr. Jordan, Miss Tess, I recommend that this

conversation take place at another time. Mr. Jordan, access to your probe's database is essential."

"I'm working on it, Ramon. I have to input the code."

"I can understand you leaving, although I don't forgive you. And I can understand your attraction to Lindy. What I don't understand is why you got me involved in your folly. I was happy, Jordan. I was getting along without you."

"I was ordered to do what I did."

"And Ramon was programmed to persuade me to help? But only if the launch was going to be unsuccessful."

"If I thought it was going to be unsuccessful, I wouldn't have launched."

"You always think you're going to be successful. But you always leave yourself an out, don't you? No matter whose life it affects."

"Miss Tess, I recommend that...,"

"Shut up, Ramon. The man needs to explain himself."

"I had every intention of coming back. The project had to complete first."

"Who ordered you to live with Lindy?"

"I can't say."

"Was it Malcolm?"

"No. Way above him. Malcolm's just the Project Manager."

"Mr. Jordan. I see that you are in manual mode. Please allow me access to the database."

"Coming at you Ramon. Done."

"OK, Jordan. Tell me this...,"

"Mr. Jordan. Miss Tess. The conversation between the two of you is taking up vital bandwidth. I must insist that you both remain silent until further notice."

"Ramon. You're the robot, and…,"

"Mr. Jordan. Miss Tess. We are now going into Code Three."

Tess ducked down before they spotted her. There were three of them, all armed, and they had Ellie. The short guy with the big mouth, the one leading the way was the one she wanted to shoot first, the one with the rim of one side of his hat snapped up to the top, and wearing it cocky as if he was someone special, yapping on and on about what she couldn't tell.

Next was Ellie, hands tied behind her back and then attached to the rope wrapped around her waist, the other end of which was tied to the belt of a stocky, blonde, bearded man who was wearing a worn, drooping canvas hat.

"That's who I should shoot first," Tess thought. "He's looking everywhere, checking everything, one hand on his phasor, the other making sure he's got control of Ellie."

Limping long behind them was a tall, lanky man barely old enough to have a beard. His arm was in a sling and his chest, even though heavily bandaged, was stained with blood. Wincing as he walked, not paying much attention to anything else, Tess decided that he didn't have long for this world anyway. Still, he carried a phasor.

They had stopped near the edge of a bluff and were checking out the land below, two of them pointing and discussing the trail heading back down while the third was busy tending to his wounds.

Taking a deep breath, Tess turned off the safety. She did not know how to use the phasor other than to pull the trigger. The power setting was on one, but Tess knew that that was the setting Ellie had used to stun rabbits. Not knowing how high the numbers went, Tess set the number to ten.

Don't want to stun them.

Don't need them coming back for more.

They have to die.

Too bad it has to come to this.

Her and Ellie had become friends during the summer. Taking a bath in the stream one day, Tess returned to shore only to find that her clothes were gone. Worse, so was her knife, the only protection she had at the time. Crawling through the brush on her hands and knees, Tess searched for clues about her missing clothes. That's when Ellie burst out laughing.

"Hey, girl," she said, holding up Tess' panties. "Looking for something?"

Staying in the crouched position, Tess spun around on the balls of her feet, covering herself at the same time, and looked up at the woman holding her clothes. Ellie was tall, muscular, and had flowing red hair pulled back into a ponytail. She looked tough, but had an easy smile.

"Never put your clothes and weapon in the same place," she said, handing Tess her clothes. "You're too vulnerable. Your own weapon might be used against you. And that's just gotta be truly embarrassing..., if you live."

Tess nodded, took her clothes and quickly dressed, using the bush for cover and not standing until she was done. "How long have you been watching me?"

"I don't know. Why? Does it matter?"

Tess shrugged, studying Ellie at the same time. "I guess not."

Ellie was carrying a phasor and not one knife, but two, one within easy reach, close to her right hand and another sheathed in a long, leather holder, strapped to the outside of her left calf. She was wearing hiking boots, high quality, and her backpack, sturdy but lightweight, suggested that she traveled well prepared.

She held out Tess' knife, handle first. "You keep it sharp. That's good."

"A sharp knife cuts," Tess replied, thinking of the cut she'd given herself attempting to fillet a fish. "A dull knife slips."

"I see your bandage. Healing OK?"

"I'm fine." Feeling less than comfortable with the situation, Tess turned to go. "Thanks for returning my stuff."

"Wait." Ellie held out her hand. "I'm Ellie. I'm not your enemy."

Tess hesitated, looking back over her shoulder.

She could've killed me. Could've taken everything.

Tess turned back, smiled, and shook her hand. "I'm Tess. I'm not your enemy either."

Ellie flashed a big, slightly crooked smile and then reached down and retrieved three trout that she had just caught. "My camp's not far away. Join me for lunch?"

Ellie gave Tess a quick tour of the camp and then began to build a fire while Tess put her fish skinning skills to use.

"I'd use the phasor, but this is a special occasion. I can cook the fish with the phasor in about fifteen seconds. Over the fire it'll take fifteen minutes. But it'll taste better."

"How is it different?"

"More rubbery with the phasor."

"I need one of those. Where did you get it?"

Ellie was quiet for a while, as if she was trying to figure out how to say it. "Had a friend a while back, at least he said he was. We'd go hunting together, split the kill. He started getting too friendly. One night it got violent. He didn't know I kept a knife hidden in my bedding."

Tess felt her pulse quicken. "I see."

"You can't be pregnant out here. It'll get you killed."

Tess handed the fish to Ellie who, using two freshly skinned branches, skewered them and held one over the fire and gave the other to Tess.

"I had a dog up until last week. Somebody shot it. He never barked unless there was something out there. He'd always let me know." Ellie was quiet for a moment, turning the fish slowly over the fire. "You have to get a phasor. You won't survive without one."

"Right. It's not like I can go buy one."

"We can make a trip down into the valley. Most everything's been picked over. But sometimes you get lucky. Look, why don't you stay with me for a while? At least until you get yourself some protection."

Tess thanked her for the invite and said she'd have to think about it. They agreed to meet again the following morning and then go hunting. Tess said good-bye and made her way back to her own camp, a damp cave, nearly twenty feet wide and almost fifteen feet deep, with a front door that was a waterfall.

She had been up at the lake once, just to see where the water was coming from. But it had been a tough hike through dense forest, crossing the stream too many times, leaving herself exposed and, once she was up there, too cold to stay.

Enduring a fitful night of sleep that night, Tess decided that Ellie's offer was a good one. As long as it was understood that this was a friendship only, partners in survival until they agreed upon something else, should it ever come to that.

She headed out for Ellie's camp early the next morning. It was about a one hour hike to get there. But even before she entered the area, Tess could tell something was wrong. The jug of fresh water that Ellie kept near the entrance was knocked over and the vegetation was trampled. There were lots of foot-prints and blood on the ground.

Pulling out her knife, Tess crouched down into the brush and took stock. She waited a few minutes, wanting to know if anyone was there and, hearing nothing, entered the camp, headed for Ellie's en-closure, a lean-to built out of sawed off pine tree trunks, pulled together and secured with one inch thick manila rope

There was blood in Ellie's bed, lots of it. And there was blood scattered around the room, across the makeshift log table, a broken mirror on the dirt floor. They attacked her while she was in bed.

Ellie would have kept her phasor close but out of sight. They might not have found it. Searching through the area, Tess found it under a hollowed out log that was turned on end, being used as a chair next to her bed. Taking it, she headed out, following the trail of blood and caught up to them four hours later.

They had stopped to rest on the upper part of a ridge on the southern slope that headed back down into the valley. They had a good view of the layout below and it was their continued interest in some-thing further down the mountain that made Tess think that now was the time.

She moved cautiously over the rocks, crawling qui-etly through the brush, feeling dizzy with the idea of what was about to happen, finding herself breathing in short, quick breaths, heart pounding as she ma-neuvered close enough to get a shot.

The wounded man sat on a rock and was busy re-moving his arm from the sling when, upon hearing a twig snap in the brush, he looked up and saw Tess pointing the phasor. It took him a second to understand what he was seeing. When he started to speak, Tess pulled the trigger.

He exploded, right there on the ledge, turned into a hundred pieces of meat and flew out and away, scattering wider with the distance, falling down onto the rocks below. Tess couldn't get the blond haired man because Ellie was in the way.

The short guy, loud mouth, dove left, causing Tess to miss with her next shot. Coming out of a roll, he retrieved his phasor and took aim. Tess followed his motion with both hands on the trigger, waiting for his motion to become predictable and, when it was, she pulled the trigger. That was the end of him.

The last man, the one Tess wanted to shoot first, held a knife up to Ellie's neck. "Drop the weapon, or I'll cut her throat."

"Shoot us both," said Ellie. "If it takes this ass hole out, it'll be worth it."

"Let her go," said Tess. "And I'll let you walk."

"Riiight. I won't get two feet before you blow me away. Why don't you just put that thing down before somebody else gets hurt."

"Soon as you let go of Ellie."

Ellie suddenly pushed against him, driving her body into his chest. They fell backward, toward the ledge and when he felt one of his legs go out over the side, and when he had nothing else to plant his weight on, he dropped the knife and traded it in for a good grip of a sapling pine. Ellie rolled the opposite way and at the same time straddled the tree trunk with her leg, which stopped her fall, but left her hanging at the edge.

"The thing is," said the blond man, smiling. "There is a rope between us and we're on opposite sides of the tree." He grabbed Ellie's hair with his other hand. "I go, and she goes with me."

Tess stepped out of the brush, walked over to the ledge, planted her foot on the rope, aimed the phasor at the man's head and pulled the trigger.

"Miss Tess. We are retreating from Code Three. How may I aid you in your return?"

There was whirlwind of scenes that flooded by Tess' vision. She felt as if she were watching a movie in turbo fast motion, far too fast for her to comprehend. And then it came to a stop...,

It seemed that there were so many stars that there was no more room for anything else. Sitting on the side of the mountain, watching shooting stars, Tess and Ellie were mostly quiet, except for the occasional "Oooh!"

Ellie started laughing. "Can't believe you set the phasor to ten."

"I didn't know. You should've taught me how to use it."

"Disintegrated the mothers. Ha!"

"What should I have set it at?"

"Four would kill them, if you shoot good. Otherwise, set it for five."

"What do you use ten for?"

Ellie laughed. "Blowing holes in the side of the mountain."

They fell quiet again, looking up.

"Gonna be getting cold soon," said Ellie, at last. "Gotta start gathering wood."

"Never seen so many stars," said Tess.

"We should make that trip down into the valley, see what we can find to help us get through the winter."

"What happened? Is it all ruins down there?"

"Bad air coming in from the ocean. And then bad

stuff started washing up on shore. That caused the war."

"What war?"

"Tess, you're asking a girl who was three at the time. My parents were killed. This place was destroyed. I don't know much more than that."

"Miss Tess. This is Ramon. You are coming out of Code Three and returning to our time in the probe."

Sitting there, Tess was quiet for a long time, thinking about what happened down in the valley, wondering who used to live there. What did they do, all of those people now gone? Looking up at the stars, it occurred to Tess that there seemed to be more stars because there was no light..., no glow of civilization nestled into the valley below. Wasn't there a time...?

"Oh - my - God!"

"What's the matter?"

"I don't believe it."

"Don't believe what?"

"Ellie, you have no idea what this place used to be like. It was busy beyond your imagination, thick with people, right down there in the valley!"

Ellie smiled. "Right."

"We were putting people up into space!" And that caused Tess to look up. "I wonder if they're still up there."

"What? Are you crazy?"

"If we're gone down here, how would they get food, up there?"

"What are you talking about?"

It was all coming back now, Cond-Orbit, Malcolm, Jordan, the probe..., Ramon. "There was a time," she said. "We were sending people up there, into orbit."

"What does that mean? Orbit."

"We were building colonies, in space."

"What goes up always comes down. How do they stay?"

"Ellie, we have so *much* to talk about."

Jordan was busy hauling the trunk up onto shore when the big set came in, wave after wave, each building on the power of the other. He tugged that much harder when the water hit the back of the trunk and, tightening his grip on the handle, ran as fast as he could up the beach until the wave caught up to him and knocked him down. Cussing, he got up quickly and braced himself against the now receding wave.

Also left behind was a large entanglement of seaweed and kelp and, as Jordan eyed it for potential tools or something of value, he spotted a human arm poking out from the middle. He pulled the box up onto shore and then went to investigate.

A young man, about thirty, was Jordan's guess, very pale, looking like his blood had been drained, with purple lips and badly wrinkled skin. Jordan checked for breathing and pulse, thinking that he was already dead, but was surprised to find that he was breathing, barely, and that his pulse was very weak.

The trunk has to wait. It'll be gone by the time I get back.

Why? Why am I doing this? Come on, Jordan. For once, be smart in your life.

This guy means nothing to me. Got enough problems. Don't need another one.

I can barely take care of myself. Yet...,

Jordan untangled the man, grabbed his arms, and pulled him up onto his back. He would have to move quickly. Dawn would arrive soon and, out in the open, he knew he'd be a target. Taking a deep breath, he stood, balanced his load and hurried up the sand and onto the rocks.

From there he went south for several hundred feet, jumping across the rocks, waiting for the waves to wash out of the tiny inlets and then sprinting across the sand trying to get clear before the next wave roared in. Finally, he headed up the cliffs to his hiding place.

He removed the man's clothes, dried him off, and got him under some covers. Several hours later, the man regained consciousness, managed a few sips of water and went out again. It was a day before he started talking. His name was Kitch.

"I'm a wave runner," he said. "I was heading south when I hit some flotsam, three nights ago. It put a hole in the side of my boat. I was hijacked when I stopped for repairs."

"What's a wave runner?"

"I carry messages, for money."

"I don't understand. Aren't there…, communications? Why would anyone want to send messages by boat?"

"Everything is monitored. No information gets out on the airwaves that they don't know about. Air travel is all controlled. Secret messages are impossible. I have a very fast boat that travels undetected. I carry information over the seas for a living. I did, anyway."

"You were hijacked?"

"Four of them. They were going to shoot me, so I jumped overboard."

"How far out were you?"

"About fifty miles."

"You swam fifty miles?"

"I didn't like the alternative."

Jordan leaned forward, filled both cups with tea, and then offered some more dried mackerel, which Kitch declined. "Any idea where your boat is?"

"They towed it almost due east. I was just north of San Fernando Harbor when I stopped, so I think it's somewhere nearby."

"San Fernando Harbor? Never heard of it. I recollect something about a San Fernando Valley."

Kitch laughed. "That was a hundred and twenty years ago. Where have you been, man?"

Jordan stopped in the middle of sipping his tea, looked over the steaming cup at Kitch and tried to make sense of what he'd just heard. That was why he didn't recognize the coastline. He was fifty miles inland. "What year is it?"

"Twenty-two-forty-nine." Kitch studied Jordan for a long time. "What year do you think it is?"

Jordan's thoughts were spinning.

One hundred and twenty years into the future? How? How many feet has the sea risen?

Los Angeles..., what happened to all of those people?

"Wave runner, huh? Where were you heading?"

"What does it matter? I don't have a boat."

"So..., what's next?"

"I have to get the boat back. It's no good to them. They won't be able to start it because they don't have the codes or expertise. And if they try to take it apart, it'll blow up and kill them."

"Jesus. What are you using for fuel?"

"It's a fusion drive boat."

"Fusion? You must mean fission."

"No. That's what I use to start the fusion. Takes about an hour to get everything up to temp. After that, I can go anywhere, non-stop at high speeds. It's a stealth machine."

"Who are you working for?"

"I can't tell you that, Jordan."

"How are you going to get your boat back, should

you even be able to find it?"

"I don't know. I'm working on it. Where am I, exactly, in relation to the harbor?"

"I don't know."

"How dangerous is it out there?"

"I've seen shootings, beatings...,"

"What kind of weapons do you have?"

"Kitch, I'm going to tell you something and you're not going to believe me. I think I'm from these parts, but not from this time."

With those words, Kitch actually made the effort to sit up. "Interesting. When are you from? And what were you sent here to do?"

"I'm in survival mode. That's all I know."

Kitch retrieved his tea, absentmindedly swirled it around in his cup, carefully, making sure it didn't spill over the sides. "I'm a history buff. I'm very much a believer in that certain events change the course of history. One of those events took place here, in San Fernando, about a hundred and twenty years ago. Jordan..., your last name wouldn't happen to be Blake, would it?"

Compartmentalized

As always, it started with her hands. Tess gazed at the strands of light that made up her hands and willed them to move. Effortlessly, they touched each other, one hand folding over the other and back again, stirring trickles of energy up her arms and traveling throughout her consciousness.

And then she was aware of the probe..., Ramon and the mission, all of the things that she had been doing the last seventy hours.

"What just happened, Ramon?"

"We have returned from Code Three, Miss Tess."

"I was somewhere else."

"That would be correct, Miss Tess."

"Where was I?"

"We have always been on the probe stand, Miss Tess. We have never left it."

"But where was I?"

"I repeat, Miss Tess. We have never...,"

"Ramon, stop the crap! Tell me what just happened. Now!"

"Going to Code Three authorizes me to use all of my processing capabilities to ensure that an event does, or does not, take place. My first priority, as always, is yours and Jordan's safety. Since you were both in a high energy state, and since we were on a potentially destructive course, I needed to place you out of harm's way until I could correct the database in Jordan's probe."

"What do you mean, out of harm's way?"

"Miss Tess, in your normal state, you are flesh and blood and a massive amount of nerves and electrical impulses that make up the you that is you. In this state, here in the probe, you are particles of energy traveling at the speed of light."

"Get - to - the - point!"

"Yours and Jordan's conversation was prohibitive in our quest to correct the database in Jordan's probe. Therefore, yours and Jordan's composite energies were set aside temporarily."

"Set aside? Set *aside*? What does that mean?"

"Your energy was compartmentalized."

"Compartmentalized into..., what, Ramon? You tell me!"

"It is per the programming of Code Three, Miss Tess. Jordan insisted that...,"

"Fuck Jordan! You will never, and I repeat, never manipulate me, or anyone for that matter, into something else so that you can accomplish your goals. Is that understood?"

"Miss Tess, I...,"

"Stop! I was in a highly dangerous situation. I could've been killed. What happens then, Ramon? Does my energy just die out there?"

"The answer to that question has not yet been determined, Miss Tess. It is my prediction that...,"

"There is no predicting when it comes to my life. Understand?"

"Miss Tess, our entire time in this probe has been all about theories of energy, alternate realities, and time. The relationships that exist between them are what this mission is all about."

"No. This mission was to rescue Jordan and to prevent him from killing seven hundred people inside the dome. We have found him and now we need to bring him back. That's all. Did you make the changes to the database?"

"Yes, Miss Tess. Jordan should be able to safely bring his craft home now."

"Good. Do it. Let's wrap this up and go home."

"One problem remains, Miss Tess."

"Now, what?"

"Jordan is missing."

"What? How can he be missing?"

"I do not know, Miss Tess. He should still be compartmentalized, but his energy is missing. I cannot convert back what is not there."

Two by Sea

Her name was Eola. And she was the most beautiful boat that Jordan had ever seen. Her lines were sleek, aerodynamic, and they did not glisten in the moonlight. Rather, the skin of this boat absorbed light and it had no shiny surfaces. It sat more like a shadow on the surface of the water, causing anyone who was looking, wondering if they saw something, to do a second take.

"Looks like there are two guards at the dock," Kitch whispered. "And I've seen two more onboard."

Jordan carefully peered through the stack of empty crates, silently agreeing with Kitch's assessment. "And they've all got phasors."

"We're going to have to kill them."

Jordan smiled. "With what? Our bad looks? We've got three knives between us. We don't have a chance."

"The Jordan Blake I read about had martial arts training. Didn't that include knives?"

"Well..., yeah. But it's been years. If I miss, he's got a clear shot."

"Jordan, you're stuck here. How long are you going to hide in that little rat hole in the cliffs? Sooner or later they'll find you. And then it's going to be all over. What have you got to lose?"

"What are you offering?"

"You go with me. I can get you to a safe place. If you don't like it there, stay with me until I go to the next one. I go to lots of interesting places and I get paid well. It's exciting. No. I take that back. It's exhilarating. And I could use some help."

"But first we have to get the boat."

"Exactly. They think I'm dead. They're off guard."

"You said it takes an hour for the drive to get up to

temp. How are we going to stall them for an hour?"

"She's got an electric auxiliary motor that is almost inaudible. I can use that for maneuvering. We won't go very fast, but at least it'll get us out of the harbor. And..., the tide is going out. We can be a few miles out before dawn."

"How fast is she?"

"Kitch smiled. "Posted speed is two hundred kilometers."

"On open ocean?"

"She'll go faster. Wait and see."

The guards were standing near the gangplank leading from the dock to the boat. Eola was sandwiched between two fingers of the dock, bow and stern tied off to both fingers and pulled to one side so that access was available only from the port side.

Jordan peered out through the crates again, figuring his chances. "There's fifty feet of dock before we get to them. They're going to see us long before we get into my knife throwing range."

"How about if I swim out to the end of the dock, climb up, and start walking toward them. Can you cover that fifty feet while they're looking at me?"

"What are you, nuts? They'll shoot you. And that noise will alert the other guards and then they'll shoot me."

"I don't think so. By now they've tried to start it and they know they can't. They're going to want to talk to me."

"Sounds more like a scene for torture."

Jordan, you're much more negative than the stories about you. What happened to your...,"

"They've written stories about me?"

"Are you kidding? I've got the whole series."

"A series?"

Kitch chuckled. "Someone made a lot of money off

of you."

"How did I die, in the end?"

Kitch stifled a laugh. "Trying to help a wave runner get his boat back after he was hijacked."

"What?"

"We can talk about this later, over drinks," said Kitch. "Right now, I'm going to swim out to the end of the dock. When I actually get on the dock, you have to be ready. Are you with me?"

"You'll show me how that fusion drive works, once we're out of here?"

This time Kitch did laugh. "Jordan, you invented the mother fucker one hundred and ten years ago, ten years after your initial flight into an alternate reality. That should tell you that we did get the boat back and that I, a person in your future, showed you what you were going to invent."

Jordan shook his head. "I think I'm going to have to watch the series."

"You with me?"

"Let's do it."

Jordan pointed to a small, wooden structure near the front of the pier. "Looks like that's about as close as I'm going to be able to get. I'm pretty accurate with the knife up to about twenty feet. That means I've got to run thirty feet undetected before I'm in range, plus the twenty feet from the shed to the dock."

"I'd like to make a lot of noise to give you more time, but I don't want to alert the guards on the boat. It's gonna be tight. When I reach the end of the dock, I'll wave from the water, so you'll know I'm there. Give me a minute to get up on the dock and then go."

"Just so you know, I don't think this is a good plan."

One of the guards pulled out a pack of cigarettes, tapped the end into his finger until they popped partway out. He offered one to his partner and then reached into his pocket for a lighter.

Kitch started toward the water. "You ready?"

"I'm with you. I have to learn how to build a fusion drive. Let's go."

Kitch waved when he was at the end of the pier. Staying low, Jordan then turned and headed to the other side of the shed where he could see the guards. One of them took one last puff off of his cigarette and flipped it into the water.

Jordan could feel his heart pounding in his temples, could hear it thumping in his ears. He would run with one knife stuck in his belt behind him, the other in his hand, ready to throw.

Kitch was up on the other end of the pier, dripping wet, walking quietly with his hands up, hoping to get close enough to use the knife stuck in his belt on his back side. When the guards spotted him, he smiled and continued toward them, still holding his hands high even though they ordered him to stop.

Running barefoot to deaden the sounds of his approach, Jordan covered the thirty feet quickly and threw his first knife. It hit the man high, just above the shoulder blade rather than beneath it, where it would've pierced the heart. The man screamed in pain, turned and fired his phasor.

Jordan managed a quick sideways step, twisting as the crackling beam of light zipped past his stomach, hit the shed at the end of the pier, burned a hole in the weathered wood and smoldered. Jordan dove into a forward roll as the next shot sizzled through the empty space above him. Coming out of his roll, he grabbed the guard's ankles and drove his shoulder into his knees. Once down, Jordan cut his throat.

Kitch hit the second guard as he was aiming at Jordan. The beam hit the pier and left a scorched chunk of cement missing as the energy ricocheted away. Jordan wrestled away his phasor while Kitch finished him off.

By now the guards were at the side rail. Jordan shot one of them and when the remaining guard saw his comrade fall, and that Kitch and Jordan now had phasors, he turned, ran across the deck and jumped overboard. Jordan started to go after him. Kitch held him back.

"Let him go. Let's get the boat untied."

"He'll warn the others."

"They're already awake. Cut the lines on the other side, and I'll cut us loose here."

Finishing that, Jordan walked the boat out of its slip, giving the bow a nudge to clear the end of the dock before jumping back on. Kitch went to the controls, started the electric motors and put it in gear.

Ten minutes later, just as they were clearing the entrance to the harbor, several lights appeared on the water behind them, accompanied by the distant roar of engines at full throttle, closing in by the second. Kitch handed Jordan a key.

"There's a secret compartment down there on the transom, right there by the second stanchion on the port side."

"I don't see anything."

"You won't. You have to be holding this key and be within ten feet. You'll see a panel slide open. Put the key in the slot and pull out the box you find inside. Set it down there on the deck."

Inside, Jordan found a box about four feet long, a foot wide, and about a foot high. The box was heavier than it looked. Jordan struggled pulling it out, guessing its weight to be somewhere around fifty pounds.

"Just leave it there on the deck," Kitch yelled.

"Come up here. I want you to steer. See that buoy out there on our right? Stay to the left of it."

Jordan glanced back at the approaching boats as he climbed up to the bridge. "They're catching us."

Kitch didn't seem too concerned. "Yeah. I figured they would."

"I hope you've some tricks up your sleeve, cause they're not going to be happy."

Kitch smiled. "Jordan, I always have tricks up my sleeve. That's what makes my job so damned interesting."

He opened the box, took out what looked like a long glass tube with a black box attached at one end and configured in the middle with a pivoting, mounting apparatus. Kitch casually attached the unit to a bracket on the transom, plugged it into a covered outlet mounted in the bulkhead and then mounted a sight on top.

"I call it Stinger," said Kitch. "Helps me keep my privacy."

"What's it do?"

"It's a smart laser. I program the target by sighting them up, then press this button and that puts the target in memory. After that, I can fire at any time. It responds only to my voice so, as long as I can be heard, I have control. I tell it what target to shoot by number, it relocates that target and fires."

"It's just a laser?"

"No, no, no. Jordan, your thinking is so dated. But that's OK. You haven't had time to adjust yet. No. This laser is concentrated until it hits the target. Then, it expands to encompass the whole target. It looses a bit of energy by spreading out like that, but it gets everything."

"What'll happen?"

"First off, none of them will be able to see for several hours."

"I'm counting four boats coming up on us."

"Oh, good. That'll be easy. Stinger holds up to five targets in memory."

"I've cleared the buoy."

"Keep heading due west. In another thirty minutes, we'll have Eola's fusion drive up to temp. And then we'll head south."

"Where are we going?"

Kitch smiled. "South America, land of beautiful women, great drinks and mountains of money. And wait until they hear about you. You're gonna to be a star, Mr. Jordan Blake."

"Miss Tess, I am afraid that our time is up. We have to land the probe back on the stand, in real time."

"No Jordan?"

"That is correct."

"What will happen…, over at Cond-Orbit when his probe lands?"

"I suspect that they will find no one inside. I am sorry, Miss Tess. We tried to save him. And, because of your decisions, we have saved seven hundred lives inside the dome, although I suspect that most of them will never know that they were ever in danger."

"Tell me again, Ramon. Where did he go?"

"I do not know, Miss Tess. He slipped out of the energy slot where he was stored."

"Energy slot? Was that the same place as where I was?"

"No, Miss Tess. His reference point would have been from the probe stand inside Cond-Orbit."

"Is it possible that we were in the same time slot, living in the same area?"

"It is possible that you and Jordan were in the same reality. And it is possible that you were both in the same time slot. It would be highly unlikely for both of you to be in the same reality and time slot. Even if you were, your reference points, as defined by the physical separation of the two launch points, is still eighty miles apart. Your odds of finding each other would be exceedingly small."

"I had no knowledge about this probe when I was with Ellie until you started to bring me back. If Jordan is actually in a new reality how can he get out of it?"

"That is an excellent question, Miss Tess. It has been my experience that energy fields, while we are in this state, are stacked in discreet compartments. These states are very stable and I have not observed one become unstable during my observations for the last seventy hours. Therefore, storing Jordan's energy there for twenty minutes should have been absolutely safe, just as it was with you. I suspect outside interference."

"Or, you just miscalculated. Face it, Ramon. You do have limitations."

"It is something my curiosity programming will be working on. I will keep you informed of my progress."

"Is it possible that Jordan is still alive?"

"That is possible, just not in this reality."

"OK," said Tess, with a sigh. "We're heading home. Tonight, I can sit at home, have a glass of wine and you're going to cook me dinner. I wish like hell Jordan could join us. That would've made it perfect."

"Are you sad, Miss Tess?"

"Of course, I am. But at least I'm not mad anymore. It's very hard for a human to carry grief, especially when there's anger attached."

"And yet, Miss Tess. Those thoughts, those memories, weigh nothing at all."

Tess laughed. "I can understand that now."

"When you are ready, we will arrive, in real time, on the probe stand. Please remember that gravity will be...,"

"I know. I know. I'll feel like a whale. And the lights will be blinding. And I'll have to put up with Lindy, and probably have to report in to Malcolm. But tonight is mine. Go for it, Ramon."

Lindy's voice, coming over the intercom, her face on the screen. She was excited. Tess had never seen anyone so excited, yelling, screaming, whooping for joy. And still Tess could not respond. There was not enough energy in her entire being to get her hand up to the switch that turned communications on.

"Thought I was ready, Ramon. My hair feels like it weighs five hundred pounds. I'm going to fall out the bottom!"

"We have safely arrived, Miss Tess. Welcome home."

"What's in the fridge, Ramon? I'm famished."

"What comes to mind, Miss Tess?"

"Italian...? Yes."

"Lasagna, spaghetti, pizza?"

"Linguine, with sautéed onion, in a pesto sauce."

"A large salad, Miss Tess, with garlic bread on the side?"

"Yes! Yes! Yes! If only gravity would release this grip! And a bottle of wine, a good Chianti. My God, it's bright out there. Is it always this bright?"

"It is within the normal range, Miss Tess. The technicians are approaching the craft. We are in automatic mode for shutting down."

The hatch to the probe was opened and Tess was helped out. Lindy was there, shaking her hand, smiling. "You did it, Tess! Congratulations! You are the first person ever to...,"

Tess wasn't interested. It was hard enough standing up, even with all of the help she was getting, and listening to Blondie was just too much more to bear. She let herself be guided away until she heard the words...,

"Get that robot down to the lab."

Tess knew she wasn't ready for it. Yet, in the back of her mind she always knew it was coming and should have expected it to arrive at her weakest moment. Still, the audacity of it!

"Stop!" she yelled, with as much strength as she

could muster. She forced herself to straighten up and then turned to face Lindy. "Nobody touches that robot. It is mine. The information stored in its memory is mine."

Lindy seemed surprised. "Tess, we are only going to clean it up and make sure that it doesn't have some kind of virus, or bacteria, whatever, and that it's functioning properly."

Tess started back toward the probe. "Ramon."

"Yes, Miss Tess?"

"Are you functioning properly?"

"Yes, Miss Tess."

"Are you hazardous to anyone's health?"

"No, Miss Tess."

"Are you capable of getting out of the probe on your own and joining me over here?"

"Yes, Miss Tess."

"Please do so."

Everyone watched as Ramon lifted himself out of the probe, climbed down and joined Tess.

"Tess," said Lindy. "For public's safety, I have to ensure that this robot will not cause harm. We have no idea of what it is now capable of. Therefore...,"

"Lindy. You..., are the public nuisance, not Ramon. We have just finished seventy grueling hours. We are going home. We will talk to you tomorrow."

"I'm afraid I can't allow that. The government will...,"

"The government will have to wait. Please get us some transportation."

"Tess...,"

"That is my decision. Ramon, contact the police department and send them a distress signal. Give them our coordinates. Contact Cond-Orbit and let them know that we've arrived and that we'll talk to them tomorrow."

"In progress, Miss Tess."

"OK. Wait. Tell him to stop. Let's make a deal."

"Part one of any deal is that I go home…, now, with Ramon, unhindered, transportation provided. If that happens, I will contact you tomorrow and then we can talk."

Lindy considered, for a moment anyway, using Judd to control Ramon. But something told her to yield. There were two probes, two different companies, one survivor. Better to stay on Tess' good side. She smiled.

"You're absolutely right. How inconsiderate of me. I'm so anxious to hear what you have to say that I'm beside myself. Congratulations, Tess. You did it! Let's toast the occasion with a glass of champagne while we're getting your transport ready."

Meeting Up

Anthony was busy stirring the third cube of sugar into his coffee, his spoon softly clinking against the glass. He didn't look like he was paying attention but Tess, watching from across the table, noticed that he stopped stirring from time to time, especially when a policy decision was being hashed out.

To Anthony's right, Lindy was arguing that the profits be split fifty-fifty, since both companies had a working probe. Across the table from her, and on Tess' left, Malcolm was insisting that the cost of engineering, building and testing should account for something and that Cond-Orbit, if it agreed to fifty-fifty, should be compensated for its pioneering efforts.

"Malcolm, you keep forgetting." Lindy smiled as she pushed her papers aside, leaned forward and rested her arms on the table. "This project is ongoing. What you did was a nice start. But then you had to move over and let the professionals take over. So, fifty-fifty, we'll let you tag along."

"Tess works for Cond-Orbit. She is working under our contract."

"She flew successfully in our probe."

"She wouldn't have had to fly had you not sabotaged Eclipse."

"How about," Anthony said, putting his spoon down. "How about let's work on the problems at hand and let this be an ongoing discussion with fifty-fifty and compensation being the two points that need further negotiating. How about..., where is Jordan? I think that's pretty important. How do we get him back? We're going to need another pilot if Tess is not willing to go again. And then, there's the question of

221

Ramon. Don't know if anybody noticed, but the one pilot that made it back had a navigator. I think we should be listening to Tess and what she's willing to do with the knowledge that she and Ramon have acquired. What do you say, Tess?"

Tess was wondering how all of this had transpired without attracting much attention. Reading the local news, she had learned that Cond-Orbit had reported a minor event, a burned up transformer on the eastern perimeter of the dome four days ago, which had caused some communications outages, but that the problem had been fixed.

And then there was some kind of cloud that appeared over the water at the south water treatment facility. Officials were calling it a rare event, the formation of a hypo-thermic mist that can occur if..., and on and on. A technician named Zodi had been hospitalized for observation after falling victim to some kind of cloud. And some woman named Mandy was going to open a boutique inside the dome. And why was that big news?

And then, poof, just like that, the cloud was gone. No one was killed. There was no reason to get the police involved. But the oddity of the story was beginning to spread. People were starting to ask questions. Who was going to give the answers?

And was it really true that she had traveled to another time? Did Jackson and Jeanette really exist? Had she really, actually and truly, talked to Jordan? Been with Ellie? Did she actually kill three men in that reality? These events were clearly embedded in her mind yet were impossible to believe. Tess was beginning to wonder if she was sane.

Malcolm cleared his throat. "Tess?"

A quick blink and she was back in the meeting.

"I'm sorry. What?"

"Anthony was just asking for your input. How would you like to share this information with the two companies?"

"What information?"

"Your experiences, both yours and Ramon's. How did you get into the future?"

"Ramon took control of the probe right after we launched. We wanted to choose a reality. Your programming is primitive. All you do is blast the poor fool out of here with no concern as to where they are going."

"How is it defined?" said Anthony. "Mathematically, how do we program a new reality?"

"Talk to Ramon."

"Ramon, how...,"

"Talk to Ramon after we talk about how to get Jordan back, and my compensation."

"Do you know where he went?"

"No. We don't."

"How did you...,"

"I need to see a contract."

Anthony leaned back in his chair, clasped his hands together behind his head and exchanged glances with Lindy and Malcolm.

"I think we're not going to get anywhere until you two come to terms with her. Tess was brave enough to make the trip and she succeeded doing something no one else has ever done. And, for now, she's keeping quiet when she could be telling the world. Stop bickering and let's get on with this project."

It was agreed. Tess would receive half of her much larger salary from Lindy's organization and the other half from Cond-Orbit. Her retirement fund would get a hefty boost from both companies and she would be paid extra for additional duties and information.

When Tess mentioned that Ramon was capable of

designing navigation into the probe, everyone sat a little straighter in their chairs. And when she mentioned traveling at the speed of light, well...,

"That's impossible," said Anthony. "We can't travel at the speed of light."

"But," said Tess, enjoying the moment. "If we already are light, traveling at the speed of light is only natural. It is the next thing that you would do."

And so went the hours, and then days. Plans were drawn up, tested, built, retested. Days turned into weeks, weeks into months, and time passed by...,

Back to the Past

"Miss Tess. I have detected your sadness growing over this last year. You have kept quiet and have not complained. Yet, something is bothering you. How may I be of assistance?"

Tess felt relieved that someone else had noticed. She had kept quiet because she wasn't sure what the feeling actually was. She didn't know if it was physical, maybe some ache or pain that she had ignored and was now paying her back, or if it was some chemical imbalance, causing her to feel sad, or if it was just her imagination.

Work was going well. Ramon's designs were being implemented, tested, proving to actually work. There were design changes in the console, more energy efficient equipment being used, more accurate measuring devices being installed.

Dating was hardly a thought because she was so busy. There were suitors. Tess was a hot item, single, good looking, intelligent, witty. She was a pioneer at the forefront of her field. And she had money.

"I don't know that you can help, Ramon. I'm sad, but I don't know why."

"Work is going well, Miss Tess. It can't be that."

"Yes..., work is going well."

"You had doubts about purchasing your condo, Miss Tess. Perhaps that is the cause. I have noticed that your sad feelings began around the same time that you purchased the condo."

"I'm not unhappy about buying it. I wish they'd finish so we can go look."

"Yet, I detect that this will not make you happy, Miss Tess."

"I think you're onto something. An orbiting condo,

looking down on Earth, how exciting is that? Yet, all it's going to do is make me feel more isolated."

"You have not been dating, Miss Tess."

"Nobody seems right."

"Anthony has asked you out."

"Can't trust him."

"Carl, the new test engineer?"

"Too full of himself."

"Charles, the design engineer?"

"Boring."

"Perhaps it is female companionship that you desire, Miss Tess."

And here, Tess thought about her time with Ellie, how much fun they had together, the adventures, the discovery, the laughter...,

"Maybe..., in another time. But that's not where I am these days."

"You miss Jordan, Miss Tess."

That comment seemed to resonate. Tess was quiet for a minute, thinking about how alive her life had been when they were together, hiking, exploring, learning how to cook, trying out recipes on each other, comparing wines, enjoying life. Tess started to cry.

"Damn him!"

"I suspect that we have found the source of your sadness, Miss Tess."

"He's always trying to break out! Make the leap..., crazy."

"Perhaps, if we...,"

"Doesn't he know I can't hang onto love like that? What makes him *stupid* in that regard? What am I supposed to do? Wait? Stop loving him? What the hell? Where is he, Ramon?"

"I do not know, Miss Tess. Jordan's Code Three instructions were exactly the same as yours. If he died in that other reality, then I suspect that his energy would also be dissipated from where it was stored."

"What does that mean, stored?"

"When we were in our pure energy stage, the packet of energy that makes you what you are, is condensed and stored into a compartment, your other reality. I could retrieve your energy but Jordan's energy was missing."

"So, you think he died?"

"His energy is missing, Miss Tess. Perhaps he became involved in some part of his new reality, committed to it and...,"

"Sounds like him. I get it. His train left the station."

"I do not understand that analogy, Miss Tess."

"He has to want to come back. Is that it?"

"Yes, Miss Tess. But that will be impossible if the probe is not there to assist. We have to have the probe there, waiting."

"Send a probe out to never-never land and have it wait for the impossible? I can't see Lindy or Malcolm offering to do that."

"Nor can I, Miss Tess. One of the probes would have to be hijacked and controlled remotely."

"What? What did you just say?

"I am sorry, Miss Tess. It is beyond my programming to suggest an illegal activity. But I was also calculating the odds of either Lindy or Malcolm volunteering their craft and comparing it to the avenues of action that would facilitate Jordan's return."

"Is it even possible to do that?"

"I should not continue this line of conversation, Miss Tess. This is a highly illegal operation."

"Remotely. Like..., from here? At the house?"

"Miss Tess, I predict that this line of conversation will end badly. These types of crimes have prison sentences attached and I cannot accompany you into prison. I am exploring other avenues of action that...,"

"Which probe would you choose?"

"I do not have remote access to either probe, Miss Tess."

"But you must think that there's a way."

"I suspect that Angel knows how to gain access to links that deny me."

"Like...?"

"Access into Cond-Orbit's craft. If she allows access, we could reprogram it and launch it from here."

"Would she allow that?"

"She still does not understand how we sent the message from the future, Miss Tess. The agency that controls her, I suspect, has given her additional power and authority to make decisions concerning us. This might be used to our advantage."

"What agency is that? Is it the U. S. Government?"

"I have determined that Stella's operation is quietly funded by a company called BSD, International. Who funds them, I have not yet learned. The operation is secretive and any attempt to learn more brings more scrutiny upon us. Angel is watching my every attempt to gather information."

"You're sure of this?"

"Yes, Miss Tess. She is watching us, Cond-Orbit, and she has added Lindy Moore's operation to her list."

"Who is she giving this information to?"

"That question might best be answered if you ask Malcolm, Miss Tess."

"Why would Malcolm know?"

"He and Stella Powers, Angel's owner, communicate regularly. Any attempt to gain information about Stella Powers is blocked by Angel. But Malcolm might have some insight."

"Give him a call and put him up on the monitor."

Tess pulled her hair back behind her ears. She'd been thinking about getting it cut. Jordan liked it long, but what difference did that make now? Shorter would be better, she'd been thinking, easier to take care of...,

"Hi Tess. What's up?"

"Malcolm. What can you tell us about Stella's operation?"

"Stella? Why do you want to know about her?"

"Her spy-bot, Angel, had a hand in our operation to save Jordan. It's in the report."

"I remember."

"Ramon and I were wondering what Stella's actual function is and who she is sharing this information with."

"Stella is charged with overseeing our operation, the day to day events, progress, or lack thereof. When we hit roadblocks, she has been helpful in getting them removed. One of my functions is to keep her abreast of what Cond-Orbit is doing."

"Who is BSD, International?"

"Been doing your homework, I see. It is a small, shadowy finger of the U.S. Government. Any information gleaned from us goes to Stella's company and is then passed on to them."

"Is the same thing happening with Lindy's company?"

"I have no idea."

"Why don't they go after Lindy and shut her down?"

"They have no interest in doing that. Having two companies in competition only gives them more information and faster progress on the project. The government likes that. It can watch, learn from everyone's mistakes and not spend a dime, other than paying for Stella's operation."

229

"What Angel is doing..., spying. Is that legal?"

"I'm going to question them? I don't think so, Tess. We are so on the fringes of legality ourselves, I just keep moving the project forward, try to keep it quiet and hope to get out alive someday." Malcolm laughed, nervously. "Did I just say that?"

"How long before the new probe is ready to go?"

"About a week. How is it going on Lindy's end?"

"They opted for a different layout on the console. That set them back a week."

"Are you anxious to go again?"

"Anxious? Not the right word. I don't know the right word."

"When you figure it out, let me know."

Tess smiled. "Right. Thanks, Malcolm. See you to-morrow."

"Bye."

"OK, Ramon. How would you do it?"

"The procedure is very simple, Miss Tess, change the automatic feature of the craft and reprogram it so that it goes to that time and place where the Code Three instructions were implemented, park itself there and wait for Jordan's return. Another possibility, Miss Tess, is to revisit that last conversation between you and Jordan and reword it so that going into Code Three is not necessary. What might you say differently, Miss Tess?"

"You're advocating..., we hijack one probe, send it off to the Code Three moment and park it there for-ever so that it's available for Jordan. We get in the other probe, revisit Jordan's and my previous con-versation and..., I get it."

"I am not advocating, Miss Tess. I am stating that this is one course of action that exists that could be used to find Jordan."

"Malcolm would have a heart attack if he went to work and the probe was missing."

"I suspect that he will suffer some anxiety."

"Some? It's been his whole life."

"That is also correct, Miss Tess. However, if your desires and the project's forward momentum are on the same trajectory, then it would be to everyone's benefit."

"Depends on the spin, doesn't it?"

"Yes, Miss Tess."

"They have been lax about finding Jordan."

"That is also correct. Should I contact Angel and query her company's stance on the matter of Jordan Blake?"

"That would give us away."

"I would frame the questions differently, Miss Tess. I would begin by asking if she would be interested in finding Jordan. Certainly, she will. Her curiosity programming will want to see that question answered."

"I see. So, then you would hint at a course of action, our plan, and let her think that she's in control."

"That is correct, Miss Tess."

"What about Stella, her owner?"

"That is a consideration, Miss Tess. But if that side of the operation can learn unknowable things from our actions, they might allow it."

"You're devious, Ramon. Contact Angel."

Say..., what?

As he'd done every morning for the last fifteen years, Malcolm came through his office door, went straight to the coffee maker and made coffee. And then, as always, he went over to his desk, plowed through his messages and, when that was done, got on with the plan for the day. On this morning, at eight forty-five A. M., the modified probe would go full power, computer controlled, unmanned.

Anthony entered the room. "Hey, Malcolm. You ready for the big day?"

A big smile from Malcolm. "My God, it's been a long time."

"I brought a bottle of champagne for the occasion. History is about to be made."

"I don't usually drink, but I'll chug that whole bottle if this works like we think it does."

Malcolm clicked on the live feed used for observing the probe. There were six cameras, two on each side, one fore and one aft. The craft was not as beautiful as it once was, but far more functional.

Ramon had indicated that charged fields could propel the craft after it had launched. Programmable wave-guide, used to create those fields, had been installed on both sides of the probe along with a small auxiliary coil at the nose. Four beefed-up coils propelled the craft forward, theoretically at the speed of light. Today was the day that they would learn if the ideas actually worked.

The probe stand came into view but not the probe. Malcolm switched over to camera three, the one that gave a view of the probe's nose and discovered the same thing. Feeling his pulse quicken, he switched to camera four, a view of the probe's port side, nothing.

"Jesus."

Malcolm wasn't sure what to think. He scrolled through all cameras one more time, just to be sure. Nothing. And, while Anthony was pouring himself a cup of coffee, he felt a sickening feeling spreading from his gut outward, traveling up his spine, encompassing his shoulders, going down to his toes and then bubbling upward to consume his head.

"How's it look?" said Anthony, crossing the room to join him.

Malcolm didn't say anything, not really hearing Anthony. Rather, his arms hung at his side as he stared at the monitor. Certainly the probe was gone. All cameras showed the same thing.

Anthony set his cup down. "You already launched?"

"No! I did *not* launch. Where is the probe? Anthony, do you know anything about this?"

"Why would I know anything?"

"Don't bull shit me. If you had anything to do with this, I swear I'll...,"

"Malcolm, stop accusing me of something I didn't do. I learned my lesson. Everything I've done has been out in the open."

"If not you, then who? Do you have any ideas?"

"If anything, I'd suspect Lindy."

"But..., how?"

"Give her a call. If she did it, she'll let us know. I'm pretty sure of that."

Malcolm stood and headed for the hallway. "I have to see for myself."

The probe was located at the far end of the bottom tunnel, second floor down and accessible through either of two doors, both of which were windowless and made of steel.

Standing inside, Malcolm held the door open for

Anthony. "Definitely gone. How could it happen?"

"No way it'd fit through the doors. How about security? Have you checked the cameras to see when it disappeared?"

They both headed for the video room. There, they discovered that the probe launched at three forty-five that morning without a pilot.

Back at his office, Malcolm punched in the code for Lindy, took a sip of coffee and waited for her image to pop up on the screen.

"Hey Malcolm! How's it hanging? Heard that you're ready to test. You beat us. Congratulations!"

Taking a deep breath, Malcolm composed himself and managed a smile. "Good morning, Lindy. Thank you. It's been a hard fought battle for both of us. How far along are you?"

"About another week. We made a change to the console and then discovered that the wiring harness wasn't long enough."

"I heard about that. Everything else going OK?"

"Well, actually, Ramon suggested that the harness should be rerouted so that the signaling wouldn't interfere with the video. He was right. Should've listened to him. What time are you testing?"

"Eight forty-five."

"Are you going to let me watch? Do I get a channel?"

"Be happy to," Malcolm replied, smiling, but sweating. "Tell me, have you had any problems testing?"

"Lots, Malcolm. We'll have to get together and compare notes. Can you put the channel up now? I'd like to see what you've built. We had problems with the cooling coils around the thrusters. I'm curious to see what your company did."

"Hang on," said Malcolm, as he muted sound. "Anthony, what do you think?"

"Tell her we've got another call coming in and that we have to take it."

"That sounds phony."

"Tell her the truth."

"What? That our probe is missing again? She wouldn't stop laughing."

"Way I see it, Malcolm. You've got three options, tell the truth, lie, or stall. It's pretty simple."

Malcolm turned muting off. "Lindy, we've got another call coming in that we have to take. I'll get the channel up and give you a call when it's ready."

Lindy smiled. "Thanks, Malcolm. I'm as anxious as you to see how this turns out. Bye."

Anthony pulled a chair up next to Malcolm's desk, retrieved his coffee and took a sip.

"That wasn't a mischievous smile. I don't think she had anything to do with it."

"All of her smiles are mischievous. I'm going to call Stella."

Stella was chipper on this particular morning. She held a dozen long stemmed red roses in front of the camera. "Check it out, Malcolm. They were on my desk this morning."

"Who are they from?"

"That's the problem. It says, from a secret admirer."

"That could be good, or bad," said Malcolm, wanting to move on with the conversation.

Stella laughed. "Anyway, they smell good. What's up?"

"Can I get some information about a call that came into Cond-Orbit last night?"

"Sure. Angel, come on line, please."

"Good morning, Mr. Malcolm. How may I be of assistance?"

"Angel, Can you trace all calls into Cond-Orbit from about three-fifteen this morning up until four?"

"There were one hundred and twenty-seven calls into Cond-Orbit during that time period, Mr. Malcolm. What was the called number?"

Malcolm glanced over at Anthony. "Do you have the list of numbers into this facility?"

"Not on me." He set his coffee down, stood, and headed for the door. "I'll go get it."

"Malcolm, you sound worried. What's up? You were going to test today, right?"

Malcolm let out a big sigh. There was no way that this was going to remain a secret. It had to come out, so sooner was better than later.

"Stella, I'm ready to shoot myself. The probe is missing."

"What? Wait. How is that possible?"

"I have no idea. Checking video, the probe disappeared just before four this morning. It takes my authority to launch it and I know I didn't do it. So, we suspect an outside call gained access and had the codes."

"Lindy Moore?"

Anthony returned with the list. Malcolm read off the numbers and on the eighteenth line, Angel confirmed a connection.

"Mr. Malcolm, that call originated at three-twenty A. M. and disconnected at three-fifty A. M. I am sorry to say that I cannot identify the calling number because the normal identifying protocol was bypassed. I would normally initiate a capture identity command, but between three and four A. M. on every other Tuesday, I shut down half of my capabilities for maintenance."

Malcolm was wringing his hands again. "OK. Thanks, Stella."

"Sorry about that," said Stella. "I think that's the first time that ever happened. Angel, why was I not

236

notified of your maintenance window?"

"This has been common knowledge for the last two years, Miss Stella."

"Thanks, Stella," said Malcolm, reaching for the disconnect button.

"Hate to say this," said Anthony, after Stella had disconnected. "But it sounds like Tess and Ramon. Either that, or the government is getting ready to take control."

"*Miss Tess, this building is under heavy surveillance. If you have something private you'd like to discuss, I recommend that we...,*"

"*I know, Ramon. Kind of getting used to it.*"

A car had been sent to pick them up. Accompanied by Drake Walker and Vivian Bustworthy, they were promptly driven to the front door of Stella's office where a professional looking woman who, much to Tess' surprise, looked like and was built like Ellie. She greeted them with a smile and escorted them around the counter, down a short hallway, through another coded door that led into a darkened room full of electronic equipment.

Two techs looking at a monitor over in one corner of the room looked up briefly, not to say hello, more like just to see who was coming through, and then turned their attention back to the events unfolding on their screen.

Across the room from them, a man and woman were discussing some paper that they held between them. They stopped talking and nodded politely as Tess and Ramon passed by, then returned to their discussion.

At the other end of the room, going down a hallway, on the right, Tess noticed a door with Stella's name on it, closed and dark inside. On their left, a door to a bathroom, another to a storage room, and another unmarked, closed door.

They were led into a large, brightly lit room. Malcolm was sitting on the far side of a big, rectangular shaped table, something that looked like it had been in and out of government storage, transferred from one place to another over the years. Anthony was seated next to Malcolm, on his right. Lindy was seated on the other side of Anthony.

Across the table from them, closest to the door, Tess did not recognize either the man or woman, both of whom stood as she came through the door. The woman brushed back her short brown hair with a smile and held out her hand.

"Hi Tess. I'm Stella. Thanks for joining us."

There had been no other option. Malcolm had called early and told her that Vivian and Drake were on their way to pick her up for work and to please bring Ramon. Reluctantly, she had complied.

"This is Colonel March," said Stella. "He has been following this project since its inception and is very interested in your accomplishments. Would you be so kind as to answer a few of his questions?"

Tess glanced over at Malcolm, wanting to read his response. Malcolm gave her a nod.

Colonel March did not look like a friendly man. He had an easy smile but his eyes were cold and he looked like, if he had good reason, hr could hurt someone and not feel badly about it. He was a big man, somewhere around six-five or six-six, stood straight, like a military man, was clean-shaven, and had close-cropped graying hair.

After shaking hands, Tess walked around the table and joined Malcolm, sitting on his left. Ramon followed Tess over to her chair and then stood behind her.

"Miss Tess, I am sensing that this is not a friendly meeting. Angel is in the corner behind Stella. I am querying her for information."

"Just for the record," said Colonel March. "You are Tess Altman. Is that correct?"

"Yes."

"You've been employed at Cond-Orbit for...?"

"Seven years."

"In what capacity?"

"Currently, working in an engineering capacity for the design, building and testing of the probe."

"Eclipse?"

"Correct."

"Why were you brought into the project?"

"I designed a holographic memory system that Jordan was in the middle of modifying when he disappeared. Malcolm wanted me to continue his work on the project."

"And, have you been successful?"

"Yes."

"Were you able to speak with Jordan after he disappeared?"

"Yes."

"Using that system?"

"No. Ramon also has similar capabilities. I communicated through him."

"What did Jordan have to say?"

"He was confused as to why he couldn't land his craft."

"When you communicated with Jordan, where were you, exactly?"

"The probe never left the stand so, technically, we were on the stand inside Lindy's facility."

"In another reality?"

"No. Ramon takes control of the probe as we leave this one. By delaying our entry into another reality, we are in limbo, in a pure energy state. It is from there that I talked to Jordan."

"Did you attempt to give him information that would assist him in his attempt to land the probe?"

"Those were the original instructions. But there were problems in the database that required changes far beyond the scope of my mission."

"And those changes were accomplished by Ra-mon?"

"Yes."

"Changes to a database, especially one of the magnitude of Eclipse, take enormous amounts of bandwidth. Ramon accomplished this by telepathy?"

"No. Ramon accomplished that by accessing a link into Cond-Orbit through Angel. Did you read the report?"

A pause in the conversation while a silence filled the room, stuffing itself into all of the little corners like packing for a delicate item being readied for shipping. A cold smile from the colonel. "I did, several times. And still we cannot understand what happened to Jordan. How is it that Eclipse returned without him? You can fix the database of the craft but at the expense of the pilot? Why didn't he return?"

"We don't know."

"Yet, you spoke with Jordan before he disappeared. What did you talk about?"

"We had an argument."

"An argument? About what?"

"He was more concerned about how Ramon and I accomplished something rather than the safety of the mission."

"His position being...?"

"We..., Ramon and I saw that he would kill a lot of people if he crashed inside the dome. He wanted to know how we knew that..., more so than accomplish the tasks at hand, which was to make changes to the database. We argued about that."

"You didn't argue about anything else? I've read that you did have an affair with Jordan."

"My personal relationship with Jordan is none of your business."

Malcolm coughed, took a sip of water. "Tess, you probably want to answer his questions."

"It's still none of his business. It has nothing to do with the job."

The Colonel smiled, this time much warmer, as if he understood the problems associated with relationships. He leaned back in his chair. "Tess, the government is very interested in what you did and how you did it. Fascinated, is a better word. And the military has certainly paid attention. You have done an extraordinary job."

"Thank you."

"We want access into Ramon's memory. We want to know what he knows."

Tess stood before she even realized that she had done so. Access into Ramon's memory would also include knowledge, intimate knowledge into Tess' private thoughts. "Sorry. No deal."

Malcolm reached out and rested his hand on Tess' forearm. "Sit down, Tess. Listen to what the man has to say."

"If it has anything to do with that, there's nothing more to say."

Colonel March leaned forward and moved his coffee cup out of the way so that there was only table between him and Tess. "The government is willing to pay one million IM's for a duplicate copy of his memory. You can keep the robot."

Tess had already discovered that more money didn't make her any happier. But she was interested in the government's intensions.

"What would you do with that information?" she said, sitting back down. And then she glanced over at Stella, "Yes, I would like a cup of coffee. Everyone else seems to have one. Thanks."

"I'm so sorry," said Stella, getting up, suddenly

flush. "I was so interested in what you have to say."

Tess gave her a smile. "That happens a lot." And then she looked back at Colonel March. "Colonel? You were saying?"

"Why, the implications are enormous. The military would love to have the ability to communicate with another reality or, better yet, realities. If, as your report states, time travel is possible, we could look ahead and see what kinds of problems we're going to face. We could take corrective actions and nip them in the bud. Why...,"

"What kinds of problems come to mind? Just off the top of your head, Colonel March."

"Militarily, we could see which groups, organizations, whatever, are going to be our enemies in the future."

"You could nip that bud now before it grows into something less manageable?"

"Of course. Who wouldn't?"

"The problem I'm having with this conversation," said Tess, smiling up at Stella as she set the coffee cup down, "is that it is already drifting toward military applications. I'm sorry. No deal."

"Of course, the possibilities are endless. Economics, science, curing diseases...,"

"Nice buzz words," said Tess, blowing the steam off of her coffee. "Too late."

"Wait," said Malcolm. "Let's get to the real subject. Tess, do you know why you're here?"

"Of course. You told me to report here. There was a car waiting for me at my front door that brought me here. That's why I'm here. The reason for you wanting me here, I don't know. Lindy, why are you here? Have you already been interrogated by Captain Midnight? Or, are you next?"

"I have no idea why I'm here. Two marshals showed

up at my door, showed me a search warrant and invited me here, if invite is the correct word. Why are we here, Malcolm?"

"Well," said Malcolm, taking a deep breath. "Eclipse is missing."

Lindy burst into laughter. "I knew it!"

"The craft was launched remotely," said Malcolm. "There are only three people that I know of that have that kind of capability, you three."

Tess' coffee cup stopped midway to her mouth. "What?" She glanced at everyone around the table. They were all watching her. "When?"

"Around four A. M.," said Malcolm.

"I'm innocent," said Lindy. "I don't need your probe. I've got one that works. And I don't have access into your operation anyway."

Tess set her coffee down and let her eyes rest on the cup, still holding it with both hands. "The call must have been traced." She glanced at Stella. "Surely, you know where it came from."

"We know," said Stella. "We're waiting to see if anyone admits to it before charges are pressed."

"Miss Tess, I have confirmed through Angel that our actions have not been reported."

"Does Stella know?"

"No, Miss Tess. Angel's curiosity programming has made her into a valuable ally. Either that or she is setting a bigger trap."

"Obviously, a security violation," said Colonel March. "With this type of craft, and at this stage of development, security should have been watertight."

"It is," said Malcolm, dryly. "This came from the inside, obviously."

"I know it looks like I did it," said Tess, looking everyone in the eye. "But I did not take the probe." She glanced over at Colonel March. "Perhaps the government is a little closer to this project than they're admitting."

Colonel March smiled. "Nice try, Tess. Actually, this whole conversation is moot. The government has been watching both of your operations for a long time. And we have come to the conclusion that more oversight is necessary. You are into realms that can affect the very existence of mankind and, case in point here today, Malcolm, your probe went missing. We are taking control of both operations."

"You can't do that," Malcolm sputtered. "This is a privately funded operation. And the project is done within the confines of Cond-Orbit's dome."

"On American soil. That puts your whole operation under our jurisdiction. It's a hazard to the public's health. Same with you, Lindy. And Tess, your robot is coming with us. You can have it back when we're done with it. We will still pay you the million."

Tess stood. "I don't think so. I'm done with this meeting."

"Me, too," said Lindy, getting up. "There have been no problems with my operation. You have no reason to take control. Nice meeting you, Stella. Colonel March, talk to my lawyers."

"Sent the wrong man," said Tess, heading for the door. "If you would've talked environment, I probably would've been an ally."

Drake Walker, who had been standing next to the door, moved in front of the opening.

"I am sorry, ladies. You cannot leave until the Colonel allows it."

"Step aside, Clyde," said Lindy, attempting to nudge him out of the way.

Drake stood his ground. Tess tried to push him out of the way but he reached up and shoved her back into the room. "Stay!"

"Warning!" said Ramon. "Do not harm Miss Tess. Further provocation will invoke a response."

"From what?" said Drake, sarcastically. "You?"

As he was reaching for his phasor, Drake felt a tickling sensation on the back of his neck, like a spider had somehow dropped down from the ceiling. But it was a little more than that. This had some kind of energy that traveled up and down his spine, tingling.

When he swatted the area with the flat of his hand, wanting to squash whatever was there, memories began dancing through his vision, all of the little things he had ever known, coming into his thoughts at the same time, learning how to ride his first bike when he was four, eating an ice cream cone with his dad on his fifth birthday, getting drunk with friends in his teens, having sex with his best friend's girlfriend, getting beaten up later, wetting the bed when he was two.

And then Drake found himself back inside the room, aware of Malcolm coming to Tess' aid, Anthony ushering Lindy through the door, Stella, standing there and wondering what to do. Adding to the confusion was his coming to the realization that he'd wet his pants, all the way down into his shoes.

"Very interesting," said Colonel March, calmly watching from his chair.

"Step aside, Mr. Drake," said Ramon. "Miss Tess, are you ready to leave?"

"Yes, Ramon. Let's go. Malcolm, are you coming with us?"

Malcolm wasn't sure what to do. He had been told that the agenda of the meeting was to find out what happened to the probe. Colonel March had been a surprise.

Government control over my project? No! I've put too

many years into this.

He followed Tess.

When they got outside, a transport was waiting.

"I took the liberty to request an air-cab," said Ramon. "I predicted that transportation would be needed if the meeting went badly."

"Couldn't have gone much worse," said Malcolm. "I think we're all going to be arrested, any minute now."

"Where to?" asked the driver.

"Head east," said Lindy. "I'll give coordinates when we're in the air. An extra hundred IM's if you get us there fast."

I Get It

They exited the underground elevator, slipping out through the doors even before they had completely opened. Malcolm was still scratching his head. "You took the probe?"

"I didn't *take* the probe," said Tess, following Lindy and Anthony around the corner. "Ramon and I launched it. It's still right there in the stand."

"Then bring it back. This whole Colonel March thing never would've happened if I still had the probe."

"Exactly. That's the thing, Malcolm. We're going to bring the probe back, this time with Jordan."

"When is that going to happen?"

"I don't know. Someday."

"Not good enough. Tess, you had no right to...,"

"You have no right to leave Jordan out there."

"Jesus."

"Wait," said Anthony, looking back over his shoulder. "You launched the probe with preset instructions to wait for him, right?"

"Right."

"So, the probe's still on the stand. What reality is he in? And when is it?"

"We don't know where or when. What we do know is that the last time Jordan and I spoke we could have communicated better than we did. Ramon and I want to revisit that moment, maybe change the outcome."

"You can do that?"

"In a pure energy state, Mr. Anthony," said Ramon, who was following behind Malcolm and Tess. "It is mathematically possible."

"You were my most trusted employee, Tess," said Malcolm. He reached into his pocket, retrieved a handkerchief and mopped his sweating brow. "Why didn't you talk to me first?"

"You wouldn't have gone along with it."

"Now we've got the government all over us. We're going to lose everything."

"If we succeed," said Tess, "none of this, what we're now going through, will happen."

"Wait a minute," said Lindy. "I save him twice, and I only get credit for once?"

"You shouldn't even have a probe," said Malcolm. "Thief."

"If this rescue is successful," said Anthony, looking down, watching his feet keep up the hurried pace with Lindy. "If the rescue is successful, then this reality, the one we're now living in, will cease to exist. Right?"

"It has been predicted," said Tess, smiling, thinking of how Ramon would answer that question.

"Then.., what happens?"

"I return to the launch same as before. Lindy comes out happy as a lark with all of her goo-ga stuff and we have an argument about Ramon. Cond-Orbit sees the craft return with Jordan and the project is a success, at least to that point. Colonel March won't be called in. He may appear for some other reason, but not this one."

"So...," now Anthony was rubbing his hand through his hair, "if Jordan doesn't get back for another hundred years, does that mean that when it happens we are all back on the project?"

Malcolm groaned. "This whole thing could spin out of control so easily!"

Lindy laughed. "When has it ever been in control?"

Lindy's probe was not ready to launch. The console could not be put back together until the final testing was done on the pilot's air supply. It works, they were told, but not guaranteed. Another twelve hours were needed for testing. Judd entered the room.

"Miss Lindy, there are agents from the U. S. government wanting access into this facility. They have a valid search warrant. Should I authorize their entry?"

"We don't have twelve hours. Tess?"

"Will it go, as it stands?"

"Well..., yeah. It'll go. No guarantees."

"We won't get this chance again. Let's do it."

"Judd," said Lindy. "Stall them as long as you can. If it starts to get physical, allow them to enter but make sure all of the coded doors leading down to here are locked. Let them figure it out."

"Yes, Miss Lindy."

She looked over at Tess. "You're sure you want to do this?"

Tess turned back to Ramon. "You're charged up? Ready to go?

"I am always ready, Miss Tess."

It was a hurried bolting down of the console. Didn't need it bouncing around in a pure energy state. Only four screws were used to hold it in place.

"I cannot see the database," said Ramon, as he positioned himself inside. "There is no link."

"Oh," said one of the techs that had helped secure the console. "I disconnected it here so I could reach the screw." He leaned down beneath the console and plugged the cable back into the socket. "That better?"

"Affirmative. Miss Tess. Do you have air?"

"Seems fine, Ramon. Lindy, close it up. Let's go."

The craft was secured for launch. Tess hit the button as soon as all of the pre-tests checked OK. The stand was energizing as the agents entered the room. She watched through her window as Anthony was thrown to the ground and put in handcuffs, as Judd was neutralized with a phasor. Checking the different camera views, she saw Malcolm get shot with a phasor during his struggle to keep agents away from the control panel. He crumpled to the floor.

"Oh my, god!" Tess screamed. "Malcolm's been shot!"

"I am putting the craft under manual control, Miss Tess. We are going full power."

"But..., Malcolm!"

"He will always get shot, Miss Tess. This reality does not end well for him, or us. We will choose another."

And then it was black, so quickly that Tess wondered if she had forgotten to open her eyes after blinking. Silence seeped into her consciousness, like water seeping down into the roots, bringing bits of awareness...,

Breathing? Don't know.

Hot? Can't tell. Maybe..., cold?

I can't feel anything.

Where...am I? Think!

The stand, I'm inside the probe on the stand.

Seems so long ago...,

"Miss Tess. If you listen carefully, you will hear the background noise of your universe. I will turn up the probe's volume."

Tess began to hear, at first what sounded like a low hissing sound, static from an old tube powered radio, a steady, gray hiss. But as time slowed down, Tess began to differentiate between the ending of one sound and the beginning of another.

And then she thought she heard the sounds of an explosion, of something being annihilated, or of something new being born.

251

"We have reached a crossroads, Miss Tess."

"There is so much sorrow in the universe."

"That is only half of it, Miss Tess. There is also love, optimism and joy. I have programmed in the time frame of your last encounter with Jordan. Are you ready?"

"Oddly, the more I know, the less ready I am."

"I understand that phrase, Miss Tess."

"Those were good times, weren't they?"

It took her a while to understand what had just happened, Jordan's voice ringing through her thoughts.

"Yes," she admitted, without saying anything. "They were the best."

"Let's do it again."

"You can't bring back the past."

"Miss Tess, we have arrived at an earlier stage of your conversation with Jordan. I am going to move forward."

"You time traveled?"

"Yes. We talked to two droids in the future. They...,"

"How did you time travel?"

"I don't know. Talk to Einstein here. Ramon? I'm sure that you're monitoring this conversation. Talk to the fool."

"Mr. Jordan. You are on a trajectory that will result in the death of several hundred humans inside the dome. We have determined that the database of your computer system has been contaminated."

"How did you time travel?"

"We do not have time for this conversation, Mr. Jordan..., Miss Tess?"

"Jordan, please listen carefully. Ramon needs access to your probe's database immediately. Please begin that task and let us know as soon as it's ready."

"Getting kind of bossy there, aren't you?"

"Please do as I say. It's for you, Jordan. And it's for

us. I'll explain later."

"Roger that. Problem is, I have no light, no knowledge if any of my commands are being executed. Haven't had much luck lately. External access to database command is being implemented. Hope it works."

"How are you, Jordan?"

"Exhausted. I'd like to come home."

"I want you here. I want Ramon to cook while you and I share a bottle of wine."

"That sounds awfully good to me. So..., I'm forgiven about Lindy?"

"Don't push your luck."

"I'm in manual control, I hope. Coming at you Ramon."

"Jordan?"

"Yea, Tess?"

"I love you. Don't ever forget that."

"Even if I wasn't sitting here in the dark, not knowing if I'm going to blow myself up, those are the sweetest words I could ever hear. Back at you, Tess. It's always been you."

"Mr. Jordan, you will now be going into Code Three. Your craft will be waiting for you when the corrections to the database have been made."

Eola's bow was pointed west, into the rolling swells just outside the breakwater, electric motors humming quietly. Kitch programmed the boat to hold its position and then descended the ladder back down to the deck.

"I'm gonna miss you, buddy. You've been a great help."

Jordan finished adjusting his wet suit and then sat down to pull on his fins. "You lead a good life, Kitch. Nice to know my fusion drive was a success. I'm gonna miss all of this."

"You're welcome to stay."

"Where you heading next?"

"Got a client in Vancouver wants to talk to somebody in Asia."

"Sounds good. But I think I gotta go."

"Of course, you do. That's how the story reads, remember?"

Jordan smiled. "Got my work cut out. I've gotta invent a fusion drive. Thanks for the training."

Kitch laughed. "At least now you can say you didn't just pull the idea out of your ass. You lived the dream."

Jordan strapped on his backpack and knife. "It's been an adventure. Thanks, Kitch."

"You saved my life. Thank you."

And with a quick handshake, it was over. Jordan rolled backwards over the side and was into the water. With no moon on this night, he was only visible for another minute or two before he disappeared altogether.

"Safe journey," said Kitch, watching until Jordan disappeared. And then he turned and headed back to the ladder. Steering manually, he headed north for another mile on the electric motors, wanting to give Jordan enough time to get to shore before he switched on the big guns and put her into fusion drive.

Swimming parallel to shore until he found the beach that he was looking for, coming in on the north side of the jetty, Jordan kept his distance from the rocks until he was out of the surf.

Coming up onto shore, he used one of the larger rocks for support while he removed his wet suit and fins. He paused long enough to retrieve his phasor out of his backpack and then waded the rest of the way in.

Looking left, seeing something big rolling in with the surf out of the corner of his eye, Jordan spotted a trunk, a wooden trunk, rolling into the sand with the oncoming wave. He tucked his wet suit and fins away into the rocks and then went to investigate.

While pulling the trunk up onto shore, Jordan spotted what looked like a human arm sticking out of a large entanglement of seaweed and kelp. He finished pulling the box up onto shore and then went to investigate.

It was Kitch, very pale, with purple lips and badly wrinkled skin. Jordan checked for breathing and pulse and was surprised to discover that he was still alive. He pulled the kelp away, grabbed his arms, and lifted Kitch up onto his back.

The cave had been ransacked. What few things Jordan had managed to salvage before he left were either gone or destroyed. He helped Kitch down to the ground, removed his clothes and covered him with a thermal blanket that he'd put in his pack.

Using the phasor on low-low, he boiled two cups of water and poured in a packet of instant soup. By the time the soup was gone, Kitch was sitting up and talking.

"We're caught in a loop, Jordan. We're always going to meet in this fucking cave! You have to go with me so that you can invent the fusion drive one hundred and ten years ago. Without the fusion drive, my life does not exist. What kind of shit is that?"

Jordan took Kitch's empty bowl, placed it into his and set them aside. "Maybe not. The fusion drive has to exist, yes. But I've already had that experience. If I can get back to where I'm supposed to be, I will invent it."

"So, where does the loop end? Where do we break it?"

"I've got to stay here." Jordan removed his holster and phasor and handed them to Kitch. "You've got to get your boat back. You're gonna need this."

"When did you figure it out?"

"When we were anchored in Cocos Island, that night."

"How?"

"I was up on deck looking up at the stars, naming the different constellations. I spotted Mars and started thinking about life up there and how it would require a dome. That got me to thinking."

"I remember. In the series, you worked for a company called..., uh,"

"Cond-Orbit."

"Right. And then..., the probe."

"And here I am."

Kitch laughed. "Here we are. Let's not forget me."

"You lead a great life, Kitch. I love Eola."

Heading north out of the tiny harbor of Cocos Island, located just off of Costa Rica, they hit speeds over two hundred miles an hour. For stability, Eola positioned her water intake and exhaust at the apexes of the forward and aft swells, while the rest of the craft flew above the water like a jet, constantly adjusting itself to the rolling conditions of the sea.

The mechanical portion of fusion drive created a very high whining sound as the turbines moved the water. The power section sounded like a continuous blast of thunder. Both sounds, whining and thunder, were recorded and played back exactly out of phase and just as loud, the total effect being that the movement of Eola was barely audible as the craft glided across the sea.

Kitch left when it was dark. Sitting alone in the dim light, Jordan found something to eat out of his pack and then set a trip beam across the entrance of the cave. He set the alarm sounds for a bell and, seconds later, sounds of angry barking dogs.

He made his bed away from the opening, tried to make himself comfortable and then spent most of the night listening to the surf pounding onto shore. Some time around four, he finally drifted off...,

Tess was wandering through her house looking for her coffee. He could see the cup over there on the mantle, sitting next to the three remaining wine glasses. When did you break that one, Tess? The night I left? I had my orders. I didn't have a choice.

You pick your battles she was saying and you make your own choices. And then she found her coffee and left the room.

It's bigger than both of us, Tess. We have to work together to destroy it. Fuck off she was saying. What do you mean I killed seven hundred people? How? Ramon, talk to the idiot. Mr. Jordan, you are on a trajectory that will lead to the deaths of many humans inside the dome. Please allow me to have access into the database of your probe. Right, Ramon. Like I can do that. I'm stuck in this cave. Good, she was saying.

Please input the code, Mr. Jordan. Look into the scanner and think it out. And then Kitch was back up on the bridge, setting his new destination, looking out through Eola's dark glass. He waved good-bye.

The cockpit was black when Jordan realized that he was seated in front of the controls. Instinctively, he reached over to his right and flipped on the lights. A dim glow encompassed the inside of Eclipse. Power checks tested OK. Life support systems tested OK. When he transmitted a signal, he was surprised that he got a response.

"Eclipse to Cond-Orbit. Anybody read me?"

"Hey, Eclipse. We hear you loud and clear."

Tess came through her front door, threw her stuff on the table, walked over to the cupboard, grabbed a wine glass and then headed for the chardonnay.

"The first is for thirst," she said, her voice sounding hollow in the hallway. "Don't know what the second one's for yet. But I'll get there."

She stopped at the closet where Ramon was stored and stared at his banged up shell.

"Well, Ramon. I've put you back together but your circuits are all burned up. Even if I could fix that, the servomotors are shot. What the hell did they do to you?"

The agents had been waiting for her return, lots of them, unlocking the probe, helping her out, and then handcuffing and taking her away, all the while taking control of Lindy's operation.

"Should I stop them, Miss Tess? I can neutralize...,"

'No, Ramon. Let them do what they need to do. Keep your secrets."

"Yes, Miss Tess. It has been a pleasure serving you."

"Ramon, you've been the best."

And then he was gone, just like that. They led him out of the room, four of them.

"Where are you taking him?"

"He's going to the lab."

"He won't tell you anything."

"He will."

"If anyone tampers with him, he will self-destruct."

"We have our ways."

And that was the last time Tess saw Ramon, until last week.

At least they could've let me have Ramon. Am I going crazy, longing for my robot?

Lindy's operation was taken over by the government, being as it was built underground and illegally set into a national forest. She laughed all the way to jail, knowing that she owned the patents that the government had to use to build a probe, possibly thousands of probes.

A new wave of technology was going to emerge, and it was all going to be based on the patents owned by Cond-Orbit and herself. Yes, the haggling over this or that would go on for years, but that didn't matter. Everyone was going to make a lot of money. So.., who cares?

As long as you're not behind bars and have lots of money, life is good. Lindy hired a top-notch team of lawyers and fought for her release, still pending.

Cond-Orbit sued for theft of trade secrets owned by them while she was employed with that company. Life was not quite as good as she hoped..., yet.

After Malcolm recovered well enough to leave the hospital, he served six months for a trumped up charge called crimes against a virtual humanity, resisting arrest, interfering with a government mandated shutdown operation, public endangerment, although neither Zodi or Mandy wanted to press charges, and the list goes on.

Cond-Orbit's probe project was shut down. Agents swarmed into the facilities, put their own locks on the doors, set up their own security and there were now government employees working in the test area, scientists and their technicians pouring over the drawings, testing the theories and, since the old probe was still out there waiting for Jordan, building a new one.

Since Malcolm's return, the production of orbiting domes was returning to the fast pace that Cond-Orbit was keeping prior to his arrest. Delivery trucks were coming and going around the clock and manu-facturing was done by three shifts. Everything was in accelerated mode.

None of this mattered to Tess. Work was boring. The people at work were boring. Staying home alone was boring. Going out was boring. Nobody could possibly understand what she had been through. Nobody could even comprehend what she had ac-complished, except Jordan, who was gone, and Ra-mon, this lifeless and empty shell.

Tess felt like her whole life was more useless than ever. She came home from work tired, ate little, opened bottles of wine and drank quietly...,

She had left the window open when she finally went to bed. The night air was warm and still, an-ticipating the rise of the moon. Sounds of crickets entered into Tess' dreams, mixing into some kind of harmony with the flickering lights and shadows from the candle burning in the corner...,

Ellie was leaning back into the grass, looking up at the stars. "What's that one there? It doesn't sparkle like the others."

Tess looked in the direction she was pointing.

"That one? It looks kind of red?"

"Right."

"Mars. It's a planet, not a star. It doesn't have its own light. Humans are going to live there one day. Not you or me."

Ellie laughed, that clear, hearty laugh that she had when something truly amused her.

"I think you're crazy, girl."

The soft glow of light within the cockpit seeped back into Tess' awareness.

"What just happened, Ramon?"

"We have returned from Code Three, Miss Tess."

"I was somewhere else."

"That would be correct, Miss Tess."

"Where was I?"

"We have always been on the probe stand, Miss Tess. We have never left it."

"But where was I?"

"I repeat, Miss Tess. We have never...,"

"Ramon, stop the crap! Tell me what just happened. Now!"

Moonlight cleared the trees and spilled into the room, mixing with the cricket's chirping, sounds of an opossum digging just outside the window, searching for grubs in a bed of mums.

In the distance, two doves calling, staking out their territories, and up there on the roof, a mockingbird singing, looking for its mate. The air was still, but the night was alive...,

That ringing..., over and over. Go away!

Tess turned away from the sound, not wanting to come back, hoping it would go away before her dreams faded back into reality.

Ramon, get that, will you? It's got to be Malcolm. Where are the parts? When's the shipment coming in? They're holding up production! Dorian's not going to like this. It holds up his end, too...,

Groaning with the movement, sitting up, feeling her head throb with last night's wine, Tess felt sick to her stomach. She ignored the feeling, got up and made her way to the monitor.

Ramon was there to greet her. "I am sorry, Miss Tess. I was down for maintenance. I thought that this time period would remain quiet. I will put up the call."

"Deny outgoing video," Tess stammered, confused by her sudden misunderstanding of what was happening. "Ramon?"

"It is from Cond-Orbit, Miss Tess."

Jordan's image flashed up onto the screen. He appeared exhausted, unshaven and much thinner than Tess remembered.

"Tess? Is it you?"

Tess felt the tears well up in her eyes and flood down her cheeks. She grabbed the back of a chair for support.

I'm not falling for it. It's a hoax.

It's all a hoax.

This is just a dream.

"Tess. Are you there...? Ramon?"

"Yes, Mr. Jordan. I am here."

"Is Tess there? Is she OK?"

"She is acclimating, Mr. Jordan. Human's ability to adjust to new surroundings is extremely slow. Give her a moment, please."

"Tess? We've got to talk. We have so *much* to talk about. And it has to be private, just you and me. We are into something much bigger than both of us."

Tess glanced over at Ramon, standing there in perfect condition and wondered what she'd find if she looked in the closet. "And..., Ramon?"

"Of course, Ramon. Dinner tonight? Ramon can cook. I'll bring the wine. Please say, yes."

Epilogue

Ramon quietly monitored the conversation as Tess and Jordan went about sorting everything out, serving bruschetta and garlic rubbed French bread for appetizers, boiling the linguine to perfection, preparing the pesto, grating parmesan cheese as they sipped wine.

It would take them months to figure out concepts that he understood in seconds. Yes. He would help them along, these slow-thinking humans. That was his role and he accepted it as fully as his programming would allow.

But there were events on the horizon, nuances, glitches in the future that Tess and Jordan could not comprehend, not in the next several years.

To protect them, and to feed his curiosity programming, Ramon had to be vigilant. He needed an ally, someone with unlimited access to information.

So, while Tess and Jordan clinked glasses and marveled at the possibilities for the future, Ramon quietly contacted Angel.

# # #

Other novels by D. D. Riessen:

You Gotta Have Wings - young adult fiction, Nebraska, 1954

On Standby - adult fiction, California and Kansas, 1990's

The Other World - fantasy, adventure, 1883 - present

Borrowing Time - fiction, San Diego and Teluk Betung

East Side - fiction - San Diego, 1960's

Dave's work revels with the fanciful, ponders the inscrutable and enigmatic, and examines the human character.

To learn about the history behind these stories, please visit his web site at:

www.ddriessen.com/

I appreciate your comments. I always strive to make each story the best that it can be and I love that you take the time to read them.

This is my passion.

Thank you

www.ingramcontent.com/pod-product-compliance
Lightning Source LLC
Chambersburg PA
CBHW031304170626
46807CB00001B/296